Letters from the Queen

A Debut Novel

MARS D. GILL

Book of Dreams, Inc

Copyright © 2020 by Mars D. Gill

Publisher Book of Dreams, Inc

www.bookofdreams.us

ISBN 978-1-7349423-0-9

Printed in the United States of America

Book cover design by Covers and Cupcakes.

*To my children and the loving memory of my grandfather:
Surjan Singh Gill*

CHAPTER 0 - MISPLACED

*"The curled line on my forehead is not from pain, my
love. A life that has endured mistakes, shrouds not a shard
of guilt, not an ounce of regret, for I have loved and risen
to tell the tale."*
Mars D. Gill

The Fall

Summit of Kauai's Kōkeʻe Mountains, Hawaii
October 2, 2013

ANNA TURNED THIRTY-SIX atop Kauai's Kōkeʻe mountains awaiting her pending life even though she couldn't rid herself of his memory. She stared at the glittering ocean in the valley, wind tousling her hair, tears dripping off her cheeks onto the letter she had written. But to what end?

Her lips twisted into an angry ball as she crumpled the letter and extended it over the cliff when a crisp and sudden breeze blew it out of her grasp. She dropped her floral bag and gasped, panting and descending the thousand-feet cliff behind the flying letter.

"Be careful, miss!" a voice shouted behind her as a twig scratched her arm. She shrieked but continued to descend.

Her foot kept slipping on the wet, muddy mountain. At the edge where ocean's bright blueness assaulted her eyes, she jumped high and secured the letter before falling into a fetal position, eyes pinched.

Tourists with selfie sticks, hats, sunglasses—the unnecessary nonsense people carried while traveling—gaped down at her.

A baby cried. A woman cupped her mouth.

Anna shoved the letter in an outside pocket, rising and dabbing the dust off her shorts.

Holding tree branches as her feet slipped now and then on the slushy mud, she climbed to the top, where she declined an extended hand and pointed away. "Party's over."

The crowd buzzed and dispersed, some shaking their head, some whispering into one another's ears but uttering nothing to her.

Another wind gust delivered a salty aroma of popcorn, making her stomach growl as the ache in her chest rudely thrust her into the present.

She carefully released, uncrumpled, and folded the letter sliding it into an envelope before sealing and hiding it inside her floral bag. Oh, her heart and the sack of stones it carried.

She was done getting over her man. Although visiting Hawaii like the other tourists, her bag contained only letters. Her smile hid her sorrow, and her words cleansed her heartbreak. She flung the bag around her head and trembled to the parking lot, wiping a stray tear but not hiding her face from other's stares. She wasn't ashamed. If any of these people were her and her words were theirs, they, too, would fight to protect them.

She threw her leg over her bike and pulled out of the parking lot bustling with squawking roosters.

Today was her birthday, a place to start again. She couldn't turn back the clock, but she could let go of past mistakes. Forgive and forget. This was her chance to be herself again—driven, accomplished, and focused. She wasn't alone in a foreign land. She came here to reunite with her core. Tension released, and she breathed easy So what if she hadn't settled down by her midthirties? Forget that! She had a life to live.

Single and strong.

Wind lifted her hair as she descended down the curvaceous mountain, and a song tore through her lips, one she had always associated with strength. When she forgot the lyrics, she filled it with humming. "Na . . . nana . . . nanannaa."

The words amplified when she turned a corner and laughed out loud, spreading her hands like a bird. "No! I will survive—"

Her eyes widened, and she grabbed her bike's handles, squeezing the brakes.

But the force caused her bicycle to wobble, and her front wheel rammed into a big boulder. She flew off her bike, landing right next to a pair of feet inside red-laced sneakers.

The Rise

An Unknown Place
Twelve Days Later

WHITE PLASTERED WALLS. The smell of alcohol. The suppressed urge to cough and rhythmic beeps from a monitor.

A short man with scant hair scribbled on a sheet of paper, wearing a lab coat.

Was I a patient? The one thing I'd always recalled, my identity, was no longer with me. The back of my head throbbed, and pain blinded me. My parched throat had a metallic, pungent taste, and my stomach churned. I had seen the room before, and a shudder slipped down my spine. All I wanted to know was where I belonged. It sure as heck wasn't in the hospital room, my prison, with this man. I coughed and choked on my breath. He stared right at me. Oh, snip! My heart raced, and I grabbed my bed's cold, steel handle and pinched my eyes shut as though that could blow him away. I should have felt at ease, but I didn't. The rings of the window drapes clinked.

His voice tore through my shut eyes. "Good morning to you, and welcome to the tropical paradise again. Not a cloud in the blue sky today."

I opened my eyes as he drew the curtains, bright light streaming into the room. "What paradise?"

He beamed. "Kauai, Hawaii. Where else?"

Ugh! No. There was a mistake. I wasn't supposed to be here. My lips bent and trembled as the doctor glided to my feet and smiled at me as if I was a child. I was a grown woman!

I cleared my throat. "What year is it?"

He raised his eyebrows. "What year is it? It's 2013. October 14, to be exact. Do you know where you are?"

I shook my head.

"Do you know your name?" He removed a pen from his white coat's chest pocket.

"No."

He nodded, staring at his pen.

I raised my head by a sliver. "I know one thing."

"What?" He neared me with widened eyes.

"I'm not supposed to be here."

He grabbed the bed's railing, shaking his head in tiny shivers. "Miss, you'll be just fine." He placed his other hand on his chest. "My name is Dr. John Lee—I'm the Chief Resident." His eyes widened. "Please don't panic."

The IVs felt like chains, and the doctor felt like a prison warden. I reached for the tubes attached to me.

He held my hands and pressed them down. "What are you doing?" When he grabbed the intercom with one hand, I freed myself from his gentle grasp and yanked the IVs out.

Blood oozed out of my arm, and Dr. Lee pressed a gauze against the wound. I pushed him away, and he fell to the floor. I gasped. A familiar alarm rang, and I shivered in the flimsy hospital gown. Ripping the other IVs out, I lifted my head, but my vision blurred, and my ears rang. A heavy load tugged on my throbbing head. Holding it, I slumped back onto the bed. Tears only amplified the pulsating pain. Whatever happened to plain old, painless crying?

He gripped my hands firmly now. Wet blood emerged from my nostril and trickled into my ear.

Nurses rushed in. Together, they pinned me down. I screamed, howled, pulled, and swerved. A pinch on my arm delivered a thick, heavy coat of darkness.

Elizabeth Who?

The Prison
A Day Later

A SONG, TOO HAPPY, tore through the beeps in my ears.

Yet the beep was too menacing, and my sorrow was too deep.

Darkness shed into a haze. A woman—the singer—stared down at my face. Dark brown hair tied in a bun. Lily behind her ear. A native woman. I didn't know her. Heck, I didn't know me.

"Good afternoon, Elizabeth."

Elizabeth who? Me? My energy had disappeared along with my thoughts of escaping. They had drugged me. A zombie.

Streaks of sunlight carved long shadows across the room.

She adjusted the flower behind her ear. "Can I call you Liz?"

"Whatever."

"You have big, beautiful brown eyes. What do they see?"

"I see a strange woman talking to me."

She laughed, and her belly moved with each cackle that vanished in a second.

Her finger traced the scratches on my arm. "Why are you trying to escape from the hospital, a safe place of healing? Look at these scars, my dear. Why?"

I batted my eyelashes. "Who're you? Are you a nurse?"

"No. My name is Hiwalani Keahi, but everyone calls me Heather." She lifted her chin. "I'm the founder of Lion-Hearted Women of Kapaa, a nonprofit organization to help women in trouble, and my girls brought all these flowers for you." She pointed behind her. "You don't have to worry—"

"Are you a charity worker?" I narrowed my vision.

"What do you mean?"

"Am I just a charity case?"

Color drained from her face. Stroking the handle of the bed, she whispered, "No, dear. I run a safe house for women, but you are like my daughter."

"Are you related to me?"

Heather's jaw dropped. "No," she whispered.

She must have thought me an ingrate, but their drugs couldn't silence the anger. The fragrance of fish and lemon filled the room, and my mouth watered as I licked my lips. The streaks of sun danced along the walls, informing me that outside was breezy, contrasting the stillness inside my jail.

I swallowed. "What happened to me? How did I land here in the hospital?"

She hardened her hold on my bed's handle. "You were in an accident, dear."

My body stiffened as I stretched my neck to get a good look at Heather. She knew more than a regular charity worker.

"One of my girls found you alongside the road. Don't you remember?"

"No. I remember nothing."

She grabbed my hand and caressed it. "You cracked your skull, but all is well, dear. Doctors are expecting a full recovery. Don't worry."

"Will I get my memory back?"

She tugged on my hand. "It should return. When? It's hard to say."

I sighed. Okay, all wasn't lost.

Heather drifted to the counter and returned with two plates. "You must be hungry. What do you prefer, the grilled Opihi or the fried Kole?" Smiling, she pressed on a button on the side of the bed with her elbow and raised me into an upright position.

I pointed at the plate with rice and clam-like fish.

"Great choice," she whispered into my ear, placing the other plate on the counter. "According to a Hawaiian folklore if a mother craves Opihi, her child is affectionate, and nothing can separate them."

My eyes widened, staring into her brown eyes as I gulped dollops of saliva. "What child?"

"*Uh . . .*" Heather fixed the wrinkles in the white bedsheet under my blanket when a nurse marched into the room, carrying a tray full of shots.

Staring at the uneaten plate in Heather's hand, the nurse said, "I can come back."

"Yes, please." Heather raised her hand and placed the plate in my lap. "Elizabeth needs to eat first."

"Has anyone claimed me?" Maybe I had a daughter who was frantically searching for me.

Heather pursed her lips. "You are not lost baggage for someone to claim."

I picked the fork, but it shook violently. "No? Nor a loved person for someone to search for?"

"No, my dear. Don't think like that." She grabbed the fork from my hands and scooped rice. "No one has come yet. But they will."

I turned my face away from the fork. "Yeah?" My gaze traveled to the green mountains visible from the window, and my heart swayed with the flutters of the palm trees. "What do the police say?"

She placed the fork on the plate. "*Ah, oh . . .*" Her gaze darted from the bed to the floor, and she shuffled her feet. "Nothing," she whispered.

My voice quivered. "Why?"

Heather sat on the edge of the bed and held my hand softly. "Police are useless parts of the community."

"Why do you say that?"

Her face turned ten degrees redder while she clenched her teeth. "They do no good—only intimidate, harass, and abuse the power that comes with the guns in their holsters."

My eyes watered, and I bit my trembling lip.

"My uncle was a policeman." She squeezed my hand. "He raised me, some would say, but he damaged me too." When she looked up, tears filled her eyes.

"How long have I been here?"

She released her grip and wiped away the moisture. "A little over a week."

Involuntarily, a chuckle slipped from my throat.

"What's so funny?"

"My life."

"I know the feeling. I have spent most of my life alone. And childless. But you have me. Consider me your mother. I always wanted a daughter like you."

I laughed more and shook my head. "You're wrong. I'm alone."

"You have one family member, the dearest of all, with you."

I stared at her with widened eyes. "Who?"

Heather played with the hem of the bedsheet.

I punched the mattress. "I said, 'Who?' "

She neared me, grabbed my shoulders, and peered into my eyes. "Your baby. You are twelve-weeks pregnant, my child."

CHAPTER 1 - TWELVE WEEKS AGO

*"Not until we are lost, do we begin to understand
ourselves."*
Henry David Thoreau

Anna Everly and the Familiar Stranger

Gaylord Convention Center, Orlando, FL
August 5, 2013

A CONFERENCE IN THE MIDDLE of a hurricane season in Florida was as odd as Anna's mind distracted from her team at the end of day one. Huddling under a giant chandelier, a new director of a sister publication flaunted pictures of her first, newly built home, vaulted ceilings, pure mahogany wood, rubbing her baby bump right in Anna's face. How dare she? Oh, but that was nothing compared to her cocking her head and asking, "What about your home, Anna? You are a decade older than me."

Sue Miller, her meddlesome team member, burst into a peal of laughter before covering her mouth.

Anna adjusted a strand of hair and crossed her arms. "I live on a wooded acre plot in suburban Chicago."

Sue's mouth widened as Anna bobbed her head. "Yeah, I have it all, tall trees and a fence in the backyard for . . ."

"For?"

Sue leaned in toward Anna and whispered, "You live in the city. What are you doing?"

Anna elbowed Sue, shoving her away. "I'm adopting two Golden Retriever pups. For them—the fence."

The pregnant director scratched her glowing cheek. "Hmm. What about your husband and children?"

"I don't use a fence for them!"

Everyone burst out laughing as Anna whisked away, mouthing profanities.

She slowed eyeing Jason Barnes smiling at her, six feet away. His blue eyes and dimples looked familiar, but she couldn't remember why. He lifted his limp hand and unbuttoned his suit jacket. The undone top button revealed a muscular chest, and heat rose to Anna's cheeks as she hurriedly smiled back and meandered to the snack aisle, playing with the locket on her gold necklace.

A strange heaviness took hold as she scanned the stale donuts. How did she become "a plain Jane" from the successful, have-it-all Anna Everly? Her plan for her midthirties was truly squashed. No children. No dogs. No fenced-in backyard on any plot, wooded or not. Heck, not even a love interest. Anna seized a donut before turning toward Jason, ready to ask him out and quell her misery.

"Don't worry about her," a familiar voice behind her said.

Anna squished the donut in her hand, the purple jelly squirting straight onto her black jacket.

Sue Miller screamed. "I'm so sorry." Her hands flew to her short, straight hair. "I didn't mean to startle you."

They scrambled for a napkin when a steady hand sporting a shiny platinum wedding band reached for a pile and handed them to Anna. With twinkles in his eyes and well-groomed face, Jason's teeth were but missing a sparkle. "Need help?"

"Thanks."

She carefully wiped her jacket as Sue took a step closer.

"I'm sorry we didn't get much of a chance to chat earlier."

"Earlier?" Anna asked, still preoccupied with his wedding band.

"Yes, we met at registration. Remember?"

Anna bit her lip while Sue's gaze bounced face-to-face like a Ping-Pong ball, and she inched closer. Anna glowered at her and sighed deeply. "Sue, can you please bring my purse from the table?"

Hesitatingly, Sue suspended her head and marched into the classroom by the hallway.

When Anna tossed the napkin aside, Jason handed her another clean one, pointing at a missed spot on her jacket.

She shook her head. "It's destroyed. But thank you for your help all the same."

He jerked his head around and winked. "Oh, I don't think it's ruined. It may be a hassle to clean, but the jacket will survive." His eyes glittered with a hint of a smile.

Sue returned holding out her purse.

"Thank you." Snatching it from Sue, she turned to Jason and nodded. "Mr. Barnes." And she bolted away with Sue's staunch shadow alongside.

Sue pointed at her jacket, huffing. "My aunt has the best tips to remove stains from fabrics." Her eyes popped behind her thick glasses as she kept up with Anna's fast march. "Even the most stubborn ones."

Anna shook her head and halted by a trash can, removing the sleeveless jacket in angry, jerky strokes. Her fashion statement had gone wrong like her instincts leading her down the wrong path. "Its days are over." She tossed it.

"What?!" Sue's eyes widened, and she frowned into the bin. "That looked expensive, and you dumped it, just like that?" She extended her palm as though the answer to her question would land on it.

"Certain stains can be removed only by the destruction of the material itself."

Sue grabbed the soiled jacket from the trash can as Anna raised an eyebrow. Sighing, Sue gently placed it back. "You directors earn a lot of money."

Anna marched away.

"Where are you going?" Sue asked.

Without turning back, Anna quickened her pace and raised her hand. "To my room."

"What about our dinner plans?" Sue shouted, steps behind Anna.

"I'm tired. Can you let the team know, please?"

"But we just made the plans . . ."

When Anna glanced back, Sue was pulling the jacket out of the trash can again. So typical.

Anna frowned and resumed as her state of mind highlighted the families seated by the babbling fountains in the atrium—laughing, cheering, toasting. She avoided eye contact even though her mind settled on them. What happened to Anna Everly who was proud of her career investments? If not Jason, she would find someone else. But the thought weighed on her.

In the middle of the atrium sat a lagoon where sluggish gators yawned. Anna paused.

A young girl in a brown uniform fed them—the sorriest sight Anna had seen so far.

The alligators barely responded, the fish clearly not delighting them as they rested their heads on their legs with droopy eyelids.

She tapped the shoulder of the young girl. "Return them to their natural home."

"Excuse me?"

Anna moved from foot to foot. "They're trapped here. You have plucked these gators from their real homes and put them on a fake lagoon." She grabbed the girl's shoulder and pointed at them. "Look how unhappy they are! Let them go."

The young girl rolled her eyes and freed from Anna's grasp. Her face reddened as she brisked away. Was she afraid of her? Did she think Anna was eccentric to ask such a question? The girl glanced toward Anna and whispered into an older colleague's ear. When that man marched toward her, fear gripped Anna. She scrambled away, holding her chest.

The gators weren't out of place. She was. She rushed down the hall to the elevators.

Forget the families, she didn't face anyone in the atrium or the elevator and only glared at her red sandals as she rose to the seventh floor.

As soon as she entered her hotel room, she leaned against the door, and her eyes welled up.

She crumpled into a ball on the floor. Thanks to the curse of an overactive memory, she pictured herself rejecting one guy after another. In high school. In College. At her first job. Her choosiness prevented steady relationships. Somehow, the perfect man never came along.

And yet the biggest shadow of all hung over her now: her childhood best friend, Desiree

Jason Barnes

A Few Feet Away from the Gators

JASON SLID BEHIND A POLE at a café and watched Anna berate a young girl in uniform. Soon after, she dashed away hiding behind giant elevator doors while a waiter tugged on his shoulder. "Are you dining with us, sir?"

Jason shook his head and lumbered to the gators, watching them get fed, imagining what would upset Anna about them. He glanced around at the people, a lot wearing the blue badges, here to learn new skills. Not him. He welcomed time away from home to percolate in his thoughts and better his marriage and fatherhood. Jason smiled through these musings at passersby he recognized, noticing the rings on their hands. Was he the only one unwilling to walk away from an unhappy marriage? Of course, not. The world was a dark place where nonsense lived. Maybe all married hands he shook were as sad as his. He sat down on a siding as his phone lit up. His wife. He silenced it. Why wouldn't he just leave? Being unlike his father was more important to him than being happy. That's why. But the fights . . . so many of them. And fear. Fear of more confrontations had long since replaced love.

He sighed and tucked away his phone as a colleague, David, approached him.

They fell deep into a conversation. Soon, David paraded a picture of a golf outing his girlfriend planned for him in Orlando.

Jason scratched his head. Getting a gift from the Mrs.?

He shook his head. Sweet memories with Isabella were vague and distant. They'd become figments of his imagination overwritten by painful conflicts—Isabella throwing yellow paint on the floor after an argument, her shouting at him in public—his wife's bountiful gifts. But perhaps, it was the institution of marriage that shrouded their love, and it perished in a slow, silent death. Or was it because he wasn't with the woman clothed to perfection in a fitted black skirt and white shirt under a soiled designer jacket, who had just stormed out of there? When David walked away, Jason sighed and sat down again from where he could see the lagoon and percolate on Anna. She wasn't just any woman he noticed in a conference. Anna Everly was an old hunger from high school that he'd never dared to pursue. She added challenge to his already-complicated life by testing his resolve that was now shaking. He suppressed an intense urge to follow her into her room and discover the source of her unhappiness. His gaze returned to the gators still unable to decipher how they could trigger her grief.

CHAPTER 2 - THE CAPTIVE GATORS

"Familiarize yourself with the chains of bondage and you prepare your own limbs to wear them."
Abraham Lincoln

The Dreams

The Shelter, Kapaa, Kauai, HI
December 2013

I WOKE UP SWEATING. Trapped Gators. Lots of them. Yawning. Morose. Pathetic. I had entered their cage and set them free. One of them bit my head.

After sighing and throwing back the covers, I marched to the bedroom window by the dressers and a rocking chair. I lifted the pane, and a whiff of white plumeria flowers mixed with wet grass enlightened me. Thankfully, it was sunny, and there were no gators. Across the property, a ladder perched against the side of the building, where a man washed the windows on another part of the resort—not Heather's shelter. Hard to believe I'd been here for two months already.

Kapaa was a sleepy town formed around one road surrounded by ice cream shops and shaved ice joints. Wrinkly green mountains on the west and the crashing waves to the east trapped the touristy town in a dome of constant drizzle and rainbows. All business transpired in its cramped corners, running north to south.

Smack in the middle, between that one road and the crashing waves, I stood, staring out of my window inside a nondescript building, one that most people missed from the road.

Our villa camouflaged well, keeping us hidden. People thought it was a rental in the Kappa Beachfront Resort. Which it was. But since Heather had opened the Lion-Hearted Women of Kapaa, it had become a shelter—a roof over my healed, memoryless head and another cloak of identity.

And the ocean hid in its bosom maelstrom whirlpools, its black, burned lava rocks, the wrath that produced Kauai and me.

As I shut the window, Heather marched in through the open door.

"Good morning, sunshine—" She halted, narrowing her eyes at me. "Oh dear! Look at your hair! What a muddle." Heather pulled out my comb from the dresser and thrust me into the rocking chair.

Before I could stop her, she started combing. That was Heather, always busy, assertive, and dominating. Shockingly more so than me.

"Are you hungry?"

"No."

"Financial reports came this morning. The newsletter you started is working, and our donations have increased." A satisfactory smile danced on her face as she slid the brush down my hair. "I am so happy. You must have been successful, perhaps a queen, in your past life."

I glanced up at Heather with wide eyes, but she shoved my head down. The newsletter she bragged about kept my mind away from the constant barrage of negativity. But Heather's stories about my life bothered me.

I fidgeted in my chair. "There's no proof to substantiate that."

"What do you mean, dear?"

"How did I become an Elizabeth at Kōke'e? Was my admission into this life a natural birth, an accident, or a murder?"

Heather's hands trembled. "Murder? I-I don't know what to say—try to be positive. Your memory will return someday. And I told you, dear, we found you unconscious behind a rock on October 2."

"That's why you said my birthday is on October 2?"

"Yes, yes. And I told you there was a note with you that got lost at the hospital." She patted my head gently.

"How convenient."

She stopped combing. "We've talked about this. Why don't you trust me?"

I clasped my hands. "Because I'm forgettable."

Heather turned my chair toward her, bent on her knees to come to my eye level, and hissed urgently. "Listen to me. You are not forgettable. Look at you . . ." She spread her arms wide. "Beautiful, talented, and driven despite the hardship of memory loss. I couldn't survive a day, not knowing who I was. Dear, wait for you to remember."

My voice became heavy. "The world would be fine without me. Face it. No one came for me, Heather. No one. Not even the darn father of my child."

"Maybe he doesn't know you're pregnant."

The floor shook, and I sighed. The construction trucks had arrived to start the resort renovation as they did daily at eight in the morning. They hollered and laughed, drinking beer and hammering. How simple their life was compared to mine?

I rose, wiped my tears, and snatched the comb from her hand, shoving it in the top drawer of the dresser. "I'm no 'Queen Elizabeth.' That monarch lives in England."

Heather pursed her lips. As though suddenly losing her energy, she lumbered by the side of the bed. I was taking her down with me. My shoulders slumped.

I opened the window again for fresh air where two construction workers wearing orange helmets cracked jokes and laughed hysterically.

I rubbed my belly.

Daily, I swore the baby was a monster because only a pitiful person violated and abandoned a woman. And that wretchedness was growing inside me. I shared my dark thoughts with no one, fearing they might judge me for hating my child, the only connection to my past.

"It is our ancestors," Heather's voice tore through my thoughts. She stood still by the bed.

"Excuse me?" I turned to her and leaned against the window.

"It's not your fault, dear. The place of your accident is cursed."

"What?"

"Have you ever wondered why there are no speed limit signs, no businesses, no restaurants on that road?"

The drilling began again. I shouted over it. "No. I never returned to that road."

Heather shifted from foot to foot. "It's no coincidence the road is barren. King Kaumualii's soul is trapped on that mountain." She marched to me and held me tightly before whispering loudly over the construction noise. "At night, the Menehune come out and perform rituals to free the troubled king's soul. He fought and lost the last battle and Kauai to Oahu's King Kamehameha." She released me. "But that's not important. What's important is that the mountain is cursed with his wrath. Your accident happened at the exact place of war."

The drilling sound stopped, and Heather paced the room. "We must figure out how to lift the curse; that's all. You will reunite with your loved ones then."

A smile slipped from my lips. It was a wonderful story, and she believed it.

Brushing imaginary wrinkles off her long, flowery dress, she said, "I will go now. Don't forget today is Last Wishes night."

When she left leaving the door of my pink bedroom open, I waddled to the full-length mirror in my room. With the driest eyes in weeks, I stared at my midsection, bloating like a balloon. My story was blasphemy. Head trauma wiped evidence of my existence, but the unborn baby remained unharmed. My spent life had been erased, the unborn life saved. A sharp pain hit my chest, and my dry eyes became moist.

At the twenty-week ultrasound tomorrow, I would tell Heather. I had to cross one night like a river separating me from my destiny.

It was a necessary formality. One night.

My heart raced.

Squeezing my eyes shut, I placed my hands over my ears to block out the noise of drilling. Silence. I went to my happy place. My oasis. A rustic, wooden cabin perched above a thundering waterfall that roared a deafening lullaby. Since I didn't know where I belonged, I pictured what a home should look like. And there it was in my imagination, my cabin in the middle of a rainforest with pearls of waters on green leaves and red hibiscus flowers. Calmness returned, and I opened my eyes.

Last Wishes Night

A Beach by the Shops
Same Day

I WADDLED TO THE BEACH, holding my belly, feeling unusually nauseated when I saw Dina standing at the edge of the beach next to the parking lot. Her lips were open as she peered straight ahead like she had seen a ghost. I touched her unmoving shoulder. "Let's get to the huddle . . . Dina?"

She didn't respond. I followed her gaze past the parking lot to a colorful row of gift shops and candy stores that sold overpriced merchandise to innocent tourists. Dina's boyfriend, Matthew, nestled with a woman and three boys.

Three boys.

All stared at his phone with blue light dancing on their faces. The video concluded in their laughter, and the woman kissed Matthew passionately. I gasped, and my hands flew to my head. The boys hardly noticed as they continued to stare at the phone. Perhaps, they were accustomed to the ostentatious display of affection.

I narrowed my eyes and looked at Dina's pale face. Did she drop out of high school despite being an honor student for this cheat? God knows what came over me. My wrath spewed like boiling milk out of a hot pan.

I raced across the tents of shops. Grabbing Matthew by the collar, I punched him in the face. "You jackass! You bastard!"

Dina's footsteps thudded across the ground. The oldest dropped the phone and hid his mouth in the palm of his hand; the youngest wept as the middle one stared with eyes wide open.

Pushing me away, the woman beside him screamed, "I'm calling the cops!" with her index finger pointed at my forehead.

Dragging me, Dina said, "That'll be unnecessary. I'm so sorry about this."

Matthew's face trembled in a spasm.

"Liz, it's okay. I'm okay," Dina whispered in my ear, leading me away from the shops to the parking lot. I glanced back at Matthew being comforted by the woman. Neither Dina nor his wife had the guts to show him his place. Dina's fingers dug holes into my arms, and her face glistened with tears.

The ocean waves roared an ominous beat. Dead seaweed and seal urine reeked in the air. A dark violet shade blended ocean and sky as one. I convulsed when my dry, cracked, and swollen feet, thanks to the pregnancy, met with the warm sand. With each step, the cracks grew a centimeter, and my slippers provided no reprieve as the sun set.

"Why didn't you call him out on being married?" I shouted in a whisper, releasing Dina's grip now that we were away from the shops.

"It has yet to register, Liz. Maybe he is unmarried."

"Don't be naïve. Didn't you see her massive ring?"

Our group sat in a circle near the sea by the ocean line. Rock piles stacked near us. No one on the island dared to disrupt them, especially us. We couldn't afford any more curses.

After nodding at Dina and me, Heather brought her hands together. "Everyone is here. Let us start."

We held hands and observed a moment of silence. The dark ocean waves roared, and the sun had completely descended. The clouds shrouded the land like a still from an old black and white horror movie. Shutting my eyes from the grim image, disparate sounds delivered a secret, rumbling therapy.

The seagulls quacked. The chatter of human voices hummed, and the joyful screams of children playing in the ocean's shallow waters crackled through. In the distance, a love song played from someone's radio, and I absorbed every moment.

When the timer buzzed, we released our hands and clapped once, signaling the start of the session.

In this rite, we shared our last wishes in a life-and-death situation, testing our dreams' potency and our hunger to live.

A girl named Samantha said, "I will not touch crack ever again." As she continued, I glanced around at the women I hadn't known until a few weeks ago, some whom I met only during such meetings.

Samantha turned to Olivia, who cleared her throat. "I'm proud to be gay and plan to join the pride parade this year."

Our gazes met, and Olivia tightened her lips and glanced away at once.

Next to her, a lady with tons of makeup mumbled, but my mind indulged in meaningless, white noise, fixated on Olivia. I felt alone, so alone.

Soon, all eyes turned to Heather. A towering figure in the group with a heart of gold and a matching energetic laugh, she didn't hesitate to pull out her the baseball bat she kept in the shelter, not to play the game, but to drive the lunatic men away.

Heather brushed off her dress, adjusted the flower behind her ear, and lifted her chin. "I want to settle down," she said as we collectively gasped.

Olivia straightened and clapped.

Heather's wishes centered on the group, and men never ventured near the spectrum of her desires. Her flower had been switched to the right ear and that meant taken.

"Yes, ladies, you heard me right. I have spent years blaming my ex for cheating and leaving me." Heather held Dina's hand. "Since then, I have learned to be strong, surrounded by you and am ready to give up control and feel weak in love again. So, if I survive tonight, I'll call Dudley and go on that first date he's been asking me about for months."

Olivia continued to clap with tears streaming down her face.

"Liz, your turn." Heather adjusted on the sand.

I glanced around the circle. Olivia quieted and stared at her feet with a pale face. Frown plastered on Samantha's face. The makeup lady opened her mouth and looked at me through the corner of her eye. No, not having another meltdown, ladies. Why would they understand my misery when I judged myself daily?

I wanted my life back. The way it was before everything happened and I got fat. I wanted to fly to a nameless place even though I hadn't a clue where. Heather's face radiated with an eternal charm.

Dina smiled at me with moist eyes. I had no friends here except for them.

"Liz?" Dina said.

"Yes. I want to be happy again." I folded my hands in my lap.

Heather's lips pursed. Why did she always react this way? I was glad when she turned to Dina. "It's all yours. Take it away."

Dina stared at Heather and erupted like the feared Kilauea volcano of Big Island, sniffling and telling them about how I hit Matthew.

They gasped at me, but I didn't care. I'd punch him again for being an ass.

Dina cleared her throat before whispering, "If I make it to tomorrow . . . I wish tonight had never happened."

"Oh, honey." Heather took her in her arms.

A tug in my heart made me want to jump out of my body and fly away like a bird. I rubbed my chest, hoping to appease the acid bubbling up my food pipe. The feeling had become painfully familiar throughout my unwanted pregnancy.

Dina's situation pressed my buttons like an unchecked toddler.

I crossed my arms and tightened my lips. Her wish should have been to dump Matthew and teach him a lesson.

Why did other women have to be so weak?

Heather wrapped up the meeting with instructions on the upcoming fundraiser, and we clapped to adjourn.

The women gave Dina loads of advice and started to disperse for the night, but I sat along with Heather and Dina. I had nowhere else to go. Like a baby, I went where Heather traveled.

"Heather, what should I do?" Dina asked when only the three of us remained.

"Follow your gut, my dear."

"Even if I forgive him?" Dina crossed her legs with a jolt of energy.

"Yes. It is your choice."

"But how can you, of all people, say that?" I asked, unable to control the words from slipping.

I sat upright and rubbed my nostrils repeatedly. Heather instilled false hope in Dina.

"I know I am a symptom of an unworthy, cheating spouse. And it took me years to shed the guilt. He should have carried the burden of cheating, not me. But I had to go through all the stages of denial, withdrawal, depression, and anger. Dina must too. There are no shortcuts, and I have forgiven him. We all have a right to hunger for love, even the depraved ones."

She turned to Dina. "And by depraved, I mean Matthew."

My hands shook at my sides.

"Are you okay, dear?" Heather moved nearer to me.

People called my lost expression a trance; I couldn't tear my gaze from the ground. "I'm fine."

"Do you feel like throwing up?" Dina grabbed my shoulder.

"What is it, dear?" Heather patted my back.

The waves roared.

Lightning ricocheted across the night sky.

"Do you need to go to a hospital?" Dina asked.

"No hospital can help her, Dina. She has forgotten what ails her heart, remember?"

The thunder gurgled as we glanced up. Wild breeze frisked Dina's hair. "Where did that come from? It was a beautiful sunset moments ago." She let go of my shoulder and held my hand. "Liz, are you sure you are okay?"

I shook my head, and my cheeks became wet. The wind blew my tears. A minute ago, I was proud to stand up for my friend. But in this moment, I wasn't sure if my fury was related to Matthew or my inner demons. "I punched him in front of his children," I whispered as Heather grabbed my shoulder. Dina never let go of my hand. "I can't help but wonder . . . Do you think my strong reaction is linked to my past life?"

Dina clasped her hands on her mouth and stared past me.

Heather's forehead wrinkled, and she released my shoulder and clutched her chest as thunder roared.
She nodded. "I'm certain it does.

CHAPTER 3 – THE MARRIED MAN

"You know you're in love with someone when the idea of them being in love with someone else doesn't just wreck you, it invades every part of your being."
Rachel Van Dyken, Toxic

Jason's Percolation

His Room at the Gaylord Hotel, Orlando, FL
August 6, 2013

JASON WINCED AND JERKED the phone away from his ear. Isabella's voice boomed through the earpiece even though she wasn't on speakerphone. She couldn't reach him for hours the previous day during the sessions at the conference, resulting in her exacerbated temper. She hadn't yelled at him when he'd called her from his hotel room that night when she was tucking the children in bed. And she always saved her temper for the morning.

While she continued shouting, he sat on the bed's edge, wearing his suit and holding his head.

Soon he opened the sliding doors and lumbered outside to the balcony overlooking the atrium.

The buzz of people chattering calmed him. Jason should have expected her spite as ten unanswered calls in two hours spelled trouble.

"What if there had been an emergency?" she asked.

"Babe, nothing happened."

"Would you prefer if something had happened?"

Speechless, Jason rubbed the back of his neck. Only after apologizing profusely did she let him go. He pocketed his phone and leaned on his room's balcony from the tenth floor while staring at the grounds below.

A toddler threw a tantrum as his mother's face flushed, and a waiter in uniform carried a plate full of food. Orange fish zigzagged in the pools.

Jason slid his wedding band back and forth on his finger. His wife's explosive call did nothing to him, and her harsh words had lost meaning. Unlike a few years ago, he bounced back from her insults in a flash.

It was Anna who had occupied his mind entirely, keeping him awake all night. She didn't wear a ring. Was she single? Did she recognize him from high school? Then again, why would she notice him? She was his best-kept secret.

Anna's Truth

Her Room
Same Day

A SHINY FILM had formed on her face when she
returned to her room from her morning run. She rushed to
the bathroom and brushed her teeth, vowing to start the
second day better—not mooning over an unattainable guy,
feeling sorry for her life, or listening to false predictions
about her future. Why did the unknown presume darkness,
anyway? She tossed her toothbrush in the glass.

After a long, relaxing shower, Anna dried and rolled
her smooth, waist-length deep-brown hair into a French
bun.

She slipped into her favorite white dress that
highlighted her slim figure and slid her pedicured feet into
her red heels, emerging out of her room with a smile.

Marching into the banquet halls, she held her head
high. She ignored the gators, the hotel guests, the bubbling
fountains, and the waft of fried eggs. Her convictions
faltered as soon as she saw him—the new source of her
miseries—laughing with his colleagues. The dimples in
his cheeks deepened, and his wedding band sparkled on
his finger: The man who had it all.

Anna spun around, clutching her chest. She didn't
understand the hold Jason Barnes, a stranger, had on her.

She marched in the opposite direction and ran into Sue.

"Join us," Sue insisted, carrying a plate full of food from the buffet. Instead of waiting for an answer, she pulled Anna over to a round table where Jason conversed with a young man.

He rose and pulled a chair out for Anna.

"I bet he opens the car door for his wife too," Anna mouthed to herself under her breath.

"Did you say something?" Jason asked.

"No." She smiled. "Thank you!"

Sue sat on the other side of Anna, and the young man Jason had been chatting with left.

"Where's your breakfast plate?" Jason asked, sitting.

"Anna doesn't eat breakfast." Sue took a big bite of her yogurt.

Ah, Sue, and the constant finishing of other's sentences.

"Guess what happened to me last night," Sue said.

Jason leaned in. While the lean fifty-year-old narrated her noisy hotel room experience, her glasses popping up and down with each sentence, a faint smile lingered on Anna's face. Jason was unaware of Sue's natural talent to revel in her misfortunes. The embarrassments people hid from the world, Sue was quick to elaborate.

Midway, he pulled his phone out but put it away to attend to her monologue.

Soon, a musical reminder played, signaling time to go to the keynote speech. They rose and made their way out of the banquet hall. As Sue went to the ladies' room and Jason excused himself too, Anna pulled out her phone and gave it a long, hard stare as though expecting it to ring. She sighed following the crowd into the main auditorium and took a seat to one side.

Moments later, Sue jumped into the vacant seat next to her, making Anna ram into the person sitting next to her.

"Where do you get your energy from?" Anna grabbed her chest and adjusted herself in her seat.

"God created me like this." Sue shrugged, and the microphone screeched, flashing a life-size image of Jason on the big screen.

Sue leaned toward Anna and whispered, "Ian noticed you missed team dinner last night. He didn't seem happy."

"What?" Anna sat upright.

Ian was Anna's boss and the CEO. But why would skipping one dinner be a problem?

Jason's voice rang through her ears. "I'm the founder of Purple Ink. Recently, I had two unpublished manuscripts in Chicago. No offers. And what did I do?" He walked to the edge of the stage and pouted. "I curled up and cried."

The crowd erupted in a sympathetic sigh as Anna fidgeted. His voice fizzled in her mind as she glanced at his perfectly tailored suit, a sleek black tie and a white shirt.

His perfect appearance distracted her. She also searched the crowd for her boss and the rest of her team. They were nowhere, and she swallowed.

"He's good." Sue elbowed her.

"What did you mean Ian was unhappy?" Anna fixed a strand of hair.

Sue patted her arm. "Don't worry about it. He knows how much we depend on you."

Anna buried her head in her hands.

Jason's voice returned. "If you're a dreamer like me, get up and follow your dreams—after you have had a big, growling cry." He chuckled. "Have the courage to work for yourself."

Anna lingered on his last line as the audience roared. She leaned back so worried her restlessness had created tension with her boss that her fingers grew numb.

Anna sighed loudly, grabbed her laptop bag and purse, rose, scurrying away before Sue could question her. She had dreamed of starting her writing business in the new self-publishing era, and Jason made it sound way too simple to make money working for yourself instead of worrying about an upset boss.

Outside, she wrote an email to Ian on her phone, leaning against the wall of the keynote hall. But before she could hit send, her gaze fell on a reddish-brown-haired woman walking ten steps from her while a crowd burst out of the auditorium.

Anna hastened, ducking and swerving, even shoving a few. Seconds later, she clenched the red-haired girl's shoulder and over the chatter of the crowd, yelled, "Desiree?"

The woman spun and gave Anna an "are you crazy" look, leaving her with her mouth agape.

A film of tears glimmered in Anna's eyes as the woman disappeared into the crowd, and Anna glanced at the unsent email on her phone and hit cancel.

She wasn't in the right frame to have any confrontation.

"Hi," an all-too-familiar voice said beside her. "Is everything all right?"

Jason's tender eyes contained an unnamed hunger and intense focus. But why? He hadn't been overly friendly with other women at the conference. He was successful and focused on work, unlike the womanizers she had met at bars, ogling over girls.

"Anna?" He stepped closer to her by an inch, narrowing his vision.

She jerked her head and licked her lips, wanting to tell him about her lonely nights and beg him to leave the world to be with her for absolutely no reason—just for fun. "Everything's fine. What's up?"

Jason stared at the floor with the wateriest blue eyes and palest face before whispering, "Would you judge me if I asked you out for coffee?"

"Aren't you—"

"Married, yes. And it's just a cup of coffee."

She was done judging love, even if frowned upon, wrong, and forbidden. "I would love to."

The Decision

The Café in the Atrium
Same Day

TWO HOURS LATER, as the sad gators slept and an atrium fountain sprayed near Anna and Jason, he fixated on two younger boys playing tag.

He laughed when they roared.

"Do you have children?" she asked. Please say *no*.

"Yes. Three boys."

Anna almost choked on her coffee. Of course, he did. "How old are they?"

"Andrew's nine, Jared's five, and Josh just turned one in July."

"Wow," mouthed Anna. He didn't hide his family. She stroked her mug. "You have it all—success, family. What's missing?"

He half chuckled, and Anna straightened her back still unable to read his expressions.

He took a moment and scratched the back of his neck. "I want to be a better father to my boys, you know? Be there for them more." His voice was heavy.

Her hand slipped from her coffee mug, and she grabbed the locket around her necklace, sliding it back and forth. Hating sipping coffee with a married man and wanting a lot more from him, she wanted to weep.

He tapped his foot under the table. "Enough about me. Tell me more about you."

"Nothing interesting about me. I work for *ChicagoGoers* magazine."

Leaning in, he said, "Don't be modest. You manage their publication and are the most sought-out editor in Chicago." He paused. "And beautiful. Are you mediocre at anything?"

She rubbed her burning cheeks, suppressing butterflies in her belly, picturing her nonexistent dream home. Her smile disappeared. Would her flaws balance out him being married?

"Do you have a boyfriend?"

"No." She cleared her throat and rotated her coffee mug.

"What about friends?"

Discomfort constricted her throat.

"Oh, come on, what about school? Surely, you remember your admirers from high school."

"Admirers?"

Jason winked. "One of them was me."

"Yeah right!" She playfully tapped his shoulder. The fountain drizzled a mist, and it pitter-pattered in a rhythm. "I had a best friend," Anna whispered.

"Had?"

She nodded.

"What happened to your best friend?"

She leaned back. "We grew apart."

He brushed his hands through his hair. "It happens."

She crossed her legs and rubbed her thumb against her hand. "I haven't discussed Desiree with anyone, and I just met you."

"Do you believe in destiny?"

She didn't expect the question.

His phone rang, and he silenced it without looking.

"No."

Jason glanced at the playground by the fountain where the boys had been moments ago. An eerie silence replaced their laughter. "Was it one of your friends from Stevenson?"

She shook her head and leaned forward. How did he know she'd gone to Stevenson High School?

"Where is she now? You should bridge the divide."

"I wish."

"Why?"

"I can't reach her." Her voice trembled. "I thought she was here at the conference, but I mistook someone else for her. Again."

He raised his brows. "Again? How many times has that happened?"

Her voice cracked. "I look for her everywhere."

"The world is a small place; just google her."

"If only it were that easy."

"It may be."

"Impossible."

"Why?"

"She's dead!"

Jason's jaw dropped before his phone beeped again, his hand flying to his head. "I've got to take this. I'm sorry."

Anna nodded and pursed her lips.

His color paled and body tensed as he said hello, strutting away.

She stared at her cup, now filled with cool coffee—a first. Grimacing, she stood, grabbed it, and headed for the black tray containing dirty utensils by the trash. She had discussed her deepest secret with a stranger and saw dead people refusing to accept friends could pass away when her life hadn't begun yet. She placed her cup in the tray and observed those absorbed in phones and laptops before returning to her seat with a thud.

The world had digitized, and friends had disappeared into phones behind texts and tweets. What about the minuscule minority who pined for a handshake or a face-to-face chat? They were doomed—the wretched, the cursed, and the lonely people. They were her.

When Jason returned, his face was long, and his shoulders had drooped. He slumped into his chair, his lips straight and chest heaving as though he returned from a street fight, except all the scars were internal.

Anna refused to succumb to depression. She clasped her hands. "Do you want to come to my room?"

She erased her slouch and narrowed her vision, but his expression was deadpan, only staring at his folded hands on the table. Ticks from a nearby clock became audible. Anna hadn't realized a clock existed until the seconds impregnated, awaiting Jason's response.

This morning she couldn't imagine sitting across from him. And now she'd offered him the boldest of invitations. How would tomorrow morning unfold if he said yes? And what if he said no?

She batted her eyelids. Every second loaded.

The Next Morning

The Breakfast Hall
August 7, 2013

ANNA'S HAIR WAS INTACT and her makeup flawless. Sitting across from Sue, she hid all the changes.

Sue cleared her throat. "I'm sorry for the early one-on-one breakfast meeting."

Sue hadn't touched the mountain of scrambled eggs on her plate. Odd. Her glasses didn't bounce on her nose while speaking, and she sat with her hands folded on the table. Her face was red, and her eyes were downcast. But the breakfast hall remained the same as everyday—too crowded and intoxicated with the scent of coffee.

"Is everything okay?" Anna folded her napkin.

"Yes. Are you all right?"

"Of course." Anna forced a smile and adjusted herself in her chair.

"You look tired."

She was tired. Exhausted. Done.

"Anna?"

"What?"

"I saw you with him."

"With whom?"

Sue rolled her eyes. "Jason Barnes, the entrepreneur."

Anna's hands lay flat on the table. "So?"

"Well, you two were together at the café. Right?"

Anna pursed her lips and folded her hands, remembering this morning. Wretched morning. Why had she asked Jason to come to her room? Where was her ego now? Bruised; definitely bruised.

"Anna?"

Anna jerked upright and sighed. Through clenched teeth, she said, "That shouldn't concern you."

Sue tapped her ring finger. "I also saw his wedding band—"

Anna crossed her legs. "You have trouble minding your own bus—"

Sue raised her hands in the air. "I don't deny that." She pointed her finger at Anna. "But this time, I need to talk to you. I'm risking my job for it."

"What's wrong?" Anna shifted in her seat.

"I have a secret—lots of them. The first one began the day I was born. I have spent the greater part of my life hiding from the world that I'm gay or that I check my front door three times to make sure it's locked at night before I can sleep. My weirdness."

Anna scratched her forehead, shook her head, and whispered, "Why?"

"I wanted to hide these truths to prove I was normal. So I married the first man interested in me." She adjusted her glasses on her nose. "We lasted one year. After that I said, 'No more.' The world had changed and embraced human differences, and there was nothing to be ashamed of."

"You bet."

"Really? You approve?"

Anna grabbed Sue's hand. "Of course! The world has changed. You know as well as I do that the *ChicagoGoers* magazine doesn't discriminate against sexual orientation. You have nothing to worry about."

Anna's body relaxed, and she leaned back as her gaze flitted over to Jason, who stood thirty feet from her, deep in conversation with a colleague.

When he caught her eye, Anna looked away and placed her hand on her face as though it could hide her.

Sue snapped her fingers in front of Anna's face.

Anna cleared her throat. "Yes, you've got nothing to worry about being gay."

"I wasn't worried about being gay."

"No?"

"I'm worried about the next part."

She pinched her eyebrows. "The next part?"

Sue pushed her breakfast plate away. "Yes. I wanted more from my life. I still do. When I joined the magazine last spring, something changed in me . . ."

"What?" Anna said, staring at Sue's uneaten breakfast.

Sue licked her chapped lips and adjusted her glasses.

Anna continued. "But there's nothing to—"

"I'm in love with you."

Anna's jaw dropped. Her wide eyes threatened to fall out. "What?"

She depended entirely on Sue, her best team member, to meet the deadlines. Her hard work was unparallel in the office. Anna now grew concerned that Sue was giving her two-week notice.

The buzz of the crowd gave Anna a headache, and she grabbed her head.

Sue's hands trembled. "Please don't fire me, but my feelings are clawing away at me. I don't know what to do but to confess, especially after yesterday—"

"Yesterday?"

"Yes. Are you angry at me?"

Sue's watery eyes were frozen, confessing a hunger as though she prayed for Anna to reciprocate. Had Anna's reaction encouraged her?

Sue spread her fingers on the table. "You are a shining light in my life. I'm fascinated by your flawless, formal clothes—the chiffon shirts and fitted skirts—and how excellent you are at your job, your perfectionism, demanding the best standard of work from us—"

Anna cupped her cheeks. "I'm not gay."

"I know." Sue rubbed her mouth. "I don't even know if I still have my job. But can I let it out? Please."

Anna folded her hands and couldn't decide if Sue's not resigning was good or bad. Keeping their professionalism alive after this conversation would be challenging and the HR—but Sue would only be in trouble if she reported her. "Go on."

"You've focused solely on your career. We've so many commonalities between us. When you give your attention to people, it's like no one else exists—"

"Sue, let me be clear with you. I'm your boss. While this conversation made me uncomfortable, I appreciate your candidness. As I have said before, I'm not gay, and I don't indulge in office romances, period. Nothing can happen between us. Okay? You should move on, and I can forget this ever happened."

Sue's eyes drooped, her color paled, and her shoulders slumped while staring at her clutched hands.

Anna stuck out her bottom lip. Her thumb played with the rest of the fingers of her hand as her heart split into two.

One half wanted to embrace Sue in a hug. Sitting in front of her was a lonely, fearful girl hungry for love, and she valued Sue's writing skills enough to put this behind her.

But their conversation irked her other half.

Sue lifted her watery eyes. "That's fair. But I can't see you hurt yourself by chasing a pipe dream."

"What pipe dream?"

Sue pointed at Jason, who ended his conversation and took a step in their direction only to shake hands with another man in a suit and tie. The famous, married entrepreneur, a father of three kids. He probably exulted getting asked out. But he had invited Anna for coffee first. They were even.

Sue waved at David, one of Jason's colleagues, a big, sweaty man in beige trousers and a white shirt.

He waved back with a grin and glided toward them with his breakfast plate. When he reached their three-seater table, he asked, "Do you mind if I sit here with you guys?"

"Sure." Anna scratched her neck while Sue leaned in toward David.

"You work with Jason Barnes, right?" she asked.

"Yes." He poked into his eggs and shoved a big bite into his mouth.

"Is he a good boss?"

David spoke with a mouthful. "Yes. Great man. Best boss. Aren't you going to eat?" He pointed at Sue's full plate.

Anna's heart pounded as she reached for the locket on her thin, gold chain.

"No. The food is cold now. Have you met his family?"

David put his fork down as though to think. "Yeah, he hosted last year's Christmas party. His lovely wife looked after us well. Beautiful family he has!" He grabbed his fork and ate more scrambled eggs and gulped orange juice.

"Nice." Sue glanced sideways at Anna. "Does he live in a big house?"

He wiped his lips with his tongue and wrinkled his eyebrows, narrowing his vision at Sue. "Yes, it's a mansion on the lake."

"Can you see the lake from his house?"

He frowned and cocked at Sue. "It was too dark in December to tell, but I'm sure they can see the lake. That man has it all: an elegant home, a wife to die for, and handsome kids. Why?" David brought a napkin to his forehead and wiped a few beads of sweat.

Maybe he shouldn't slather his eggs with hot sauce.

Sue smiled wide. "No reason. Was the house hard to find from Deerfield?"

Anna tilted her head at Sue.

"Not really." David continued to eat.

Sue's chin rested on her fist. "Lots of small roads?"

He took the last bite of eggs and hurled the juice down with a burp. "Oh, sorry."

He blushed. "Small roads? No, his house is right off Deerfield road where it ends at Lake Michigan: a large, red brick house behind a gate and tall trees, difficult to miss. Why?"

"Oh, I'm always curious where people come from."

"You sure are."

Anna pulled Sue closer and whispered, "Nothing is going on between Jason and me."

"Good. Sure. Here he comes." Sue smiled at Jason as Anna's heart fluttered wildly.

When Jason reached their table, Anna lifted her bag and marched away.

He followed her, grabbing her arm.

Freeing herself from his grasp, she glared at him and spoke in a harsh whisper. "What are you doing? People will see." She averted her gaze from his dense, blue eyes.

Jason raised his hand and exhaled. "Okay. Okay. What do you want from me?"

"Nothing. I made that abundantly clear earlier."

"Yes, you did. You threw me out of your room after inviting me in." Jason flung about his hands as Anna raised her index finger.

"I swear I found you slumped, crying. That's not a reaction one hopes to get after you know what."

Tears pricked Anna's eyes while the morning's events replayed in her mind. He'd touched her like he'd known her for years, leaving her fulfilled and recharged, just what she needed, but when she had awoken hours later, he slouched at the edge of the bed, his head buried in his hands. Her smudged makeup and untidy hair made her cling to the sheets, minutely aware of the nakedness underneath them.

Presently, Anna gripped her bag's strap on her shoulder and surveyed those around her. People chattered, and Sue gaped from across the room. When Anna glowered at her, she closed her mouth, grabbed her purse, and marched in the opposite direction.

"I'm sorry," Jason whispered, staring at his shoes.

She tapped her foot on the ground. "Does your future with me involve cheap, dingy motel rooms?"

His lips trembled as he swung his head up from his shoes, filling with glittery tears. "You must hold a low opinion of me."

"You're married and acting like a bachelor—"

"Will witnessing my love for my wife make you feel better?"

Anna blinked as though suppressing a sob. She turned to leave, and Jason's fingers dug into her arms. "Jason, it hurts."

"I'm sorry, but you're right. It hurts." He released her and strode alongside her out of the breakfast banquet hall and into the crowded hallway before pulling out his phone.

A picture of a curly-haired, tan woman grinning ear-to-ear brightened the screen.

Anna halted, grabbing his phone, and after a moment, asked, "Your wife?"

People shuffled around them.

"Yes. Her name is Isabella, and she's from Brazil. I met her at a party shortly after college graduation."

"Do you love her?"

He whispered words inaudible to Anna.

"What?" Anna frowned.

Wrinkles appeared on his forehead too. "Does it change what we have here?"

The crowd chattered, continuing to swerve around them.

"No, it changes nothing."

"Good, because I think the same—"

"That doesn't make you less of a cheater."

His face twitched, and his gaze fell to his shoes again.

Anna covered her mouth and shook her head. Had she lost her manners? "I'm sorry, Jason. I didn't mean to hurt you."

"What do you want, Anna?"

"Leave your wife."

His eyes trembled without blinking as his Adam's apple moved. Even the vein on his forehead throbbed like his heart beating on the outside.

"I didn't think so," she said and strutted away, leaving him frozen in the middle of a crowded hall.

Anna disappeared behind a group of women in business suits. His father's receding silhouette came to mind.

A shadow hung over his younger self as his father slipped out of the front door with a suitcase. Jason had rushed to his mother, who wept violently on the floor by her bed.

Currently, Jason cringed as more memories rolled.

Her red, swollen eyes. Flies hovering over moldy food he'd bring her. Him scrubbing utensils at a neighborhood diner after school to make rent. Then he pictured his son Andrew washing pots and crying.

Jason wiped sweat off his forehead as someone said his name, then tugged on his shoulder. Jason jerked his head around and looked into the eyes of a thin, young man, a student from his class, only a few years older than Andrew. "H-hi." Jason shook his hand.

"Mr. Barnes, impressive speech yesterday."

He smiled as the young man nodded and rejoined his party in a nearby corner. Jason slumped his head and plodded forward. How he ached for Anna's love, but how could he possibly leave his wife and become that dark shadow slipping out of his home?

Anna tossed and turned pining for Jason's love all night long. She struggled with the thought of his downcast expression afterward, but the touch of his fingers never left her body, even now.

When restless sleep took hold, strange vivid dreams rolled. The last one wasn't a dream at all. Under the canopy of warm humidity, the waves howled, and two little girls built sandcastles.

The emotions were uncanny even though the image was blurry like looking through a stained-glass window. Their thin hair levitated with the warm breeze.

"When I grow up, I want to marry and have lots of babies," Desiree said.

Anna sputtered. "That's absurd. When I grow up, I'll own my company and never marry or have children. All I need is you, my BFF."

They chuckled.

The giggles melted into a tick of the clock, and the moist warmth of the day transformed into the chilliness of a dry, air-conditioned room.

A bead of sweat fell from the current Anna's face and wet her pillow.

Her eyes fluttered open, and the still-dark room enveloped her.

When had her desires changed?

She reached for her phone on the nightstand, dialing a number from memory.

A familiar robotic voice answered. "This phone number is no longer in service. Please check the number and try again."

Anna ended the call and slapped her cheek three times. "I can't believe I dialed the number again," she whispered and held her head. It had been disconnected for a while now.

Desiree left the day Anna objected to her affair with a married man. Now she understood that ache, that loneliness. And hers had only one cure: Jason.

CHAPTER 4 – THE DREAMS INFORM

"All that we see or seem is but a dream within a dream."
Edgar Allan Poe

The Reality

Beach at the Shelter, Kapaa, Kauai, HI
The Day after Last Wishes Night

THE FIRST TIME I dreamed of her, the Kehau winds whistled under patches of dark gray clouds on a sunny day. Freckles. Red hair. Long eyelashes. And her smile removed all worries from my heart in a flash. I tugged on her hand. "Hurry now." The tall trees around the forest trail whooshed.

Huffing, she gripped her knees. "I'm trying, my stubborn friend." When she straightened, her smile faded, and she gaped at me.

"What's wrong?" I asked.

She shook her head and sobbed, hiding her face in her hands.

She pointed beyond me to the ground. "You're bleeding! Look!"

I turned and gasped. Blood flowed in a river behind me, but I was pain-free and stood sure-footed. I brought my hand to my head, and when I removed it, red color coated my palm. My eyes widened while Desiree wept into her clasped hands. Her image grew hazy, and my legs trembled. The waves roared around us as I frowned. "I had no idea we were so close to the ocean in the middle of the forest."

"What?" Desiree raised her head, tears streaking her face as my vision blackened.

A voice tore through my subconscious. "Liz, wake up, honey. We gotta go."

I patted my face, and a person came into focus. Heather's brown eyes stared back at me, not Desiree's. The sun's harsh rays beat down on us, and a book lay folded over me. Unable to take the glare of the sun and the shimmering ocean, I covered my eyes.

"Let's go." Heather said tapping my beach chair.

I clutched Heather's hand. "My friend. I think I'm remembering what happened."

"Really? That is great news!" Heather's eyes glittered. "We'll inform your doctor." She tugged my arm. "For now, let's get you to your ultrasound. We're already late."

"No." I swung my feet off the recliner.

"No what?"

I slid into my flip-flops. "I can't do the ultrasound."

"I can reschedule." She pulled out her phone.

I raised my hands. "No, you don't understand. I don't want this baby."

Heather's eyes widened, and she stroked her chest. "What?"

I rose, holding my book close. "Without knowing where the baby came from or how to take care of even myself or feel any bond with it, I can't be a mother."

Heather dialed as she spoke. "But you are not alone, my dear. We are here for you."

"How long can I stay here in the safe house?"

She placed the phone to her ear. "Forever, as far as I am concerned. Be right back." She lumbered away and said, "I need to reschedule . . ." into her phone, her voice receding with each step.

I waited with a knot in my stomach, hungry for support for my decision.

Carefree people sunbathed and played in the ocean. On the far corner of the beach, Dina and Matthew stood, talking at each other. Dina's wet eyes shimmered in the reflection of the afternoon sun. I prayed for her to have courage.

When Heather returned, I pointed at them. "Why is Dina entertaining Matthew?"

"He came begging this morning."

I shook my head, turning to Heather. "She should have thrown him out of her life."

"Love, my dear, doesn't listen to reason. Now, please don't worry about the baby. I have rescheduled—"

"I want to abort," I said in an elevated voice.

She gaped at me. "But you're twenty weeks into your pregnancy!"

"Legally, I can abort before twenty-four weeks."

When I passed her, she grabbed my shoulder "Liz, listen—"

I clenched my teeth, jabbing a finger at her face and freeing myself. "It's my choice! You . . . *eh*, you're always bossy and controlling. Do you realize I'm a grown woman, for God's sake! And I'm not your daughter." I bolted away toward the shelter.

Once inside, I fell to my knees and sobbed. When my breathing normalized, my heart gripped with instant remorse. Why couldn't I have told her calmly? Darn hormones. I trudged back outside as Olivia parked in the driveway.

At the beach, Heather stood with Dina, and Matthew had left. I approached them as ocean waves lapped at their feet.

Their words reached my ears before their faces. "She is so headstrong, Dina."

"But surely that's not why you think she is alone, and no one came for her?"

A cord broke in me, and I covered my mouth. Before they noticed me, I raced inside, passing Olivia at the door of the villa.

"Are you okay?" she said when I reached my bedroom door.

Suddenly, I turned, ready to vent.

But before I vocalized my misery, she blurted, "F-feel better" and excused herself.

I dashed into my room, closed the door, and slumped onto my bed, bleeding warm tears. My chest heaved, and I rubbed my eyes. For the first time, I wept for the father I had convinced myself to hate. I needed a rescue where a firetruck stopped the traffic, sped your way, and clinical experts deemed you fit to reenter the world with a clean chit of health. But no one came. And I deserved misery. Just freaking didn't know why.

Hours later when the rhythmic swish of the drapes and the music of the waves rang in my ear, someone knocked on my door, and I raised my head from my pool of tears, wiping my face.

Heather entered. "Stress and anxiety are normal in pregnancy."

The breeze through the open window played with my hair as I rose to a seated position, my chest light after the meltdown. "I'm not discussing this anymore, and I know what you think about me."

"And what is that, my dear?" She held sheets of paper.

"That I'm a bad person: Why no one came looking for me." My lips twisted.

"No . . . No, my darling. I would never think like that. On the contrary—"

"I heard you and Dina talking outside." I grabbed a pillow and placed it in my lap.

"You misheard, my dear. Your loss is my gain; you are with me because of your misfortune. And we know you're not a bad person." She gently slapped my shoulder. "Don't be silly."

"No? Not even because I don't love my baby as a mother should?"

Heather's face paled. She sat at the edge of the bed and smoothed the creases in the sheet. "I can't judge a mother, not having gone through it myself, and no, you're not a bad mother. You're hurting, but you'll overcome."

"I've googled clinics—"

"You have four more weeks."

"What?"

"Legally, you have a month to decide." She extended the sheets of paper to me. "Read through these papers. These are adoption agencies. You can make an informed decision."

"I—"

"No, Liz. Please. Do this for me."

I snatched the papers from her, but she refused to leave.

"Is there anything else?"

The drapes swished, calming my nerves.

"Can you write him a letter?"

"Who?"

"The father of your child."

"Why?" My eyes opened.

"It may deliver closure and put your tensions at ease, and who knows—it may rekindle your memory."

"Okay." I scratched my head.

Heather treaded to my dresser, pulled out a letter pad and a pen, and brought them to me.

"You want me to do it right now?"

"Yes. You told me earlier you're starting to remember. This may help."

I pulled the letter pad and pen out of her hand, peering into her unblinking, brown eyes.

"I'll leave you to write," she said while smiling. At the door, she hesitated. "We'll wait for you at dinner. It'll be ready in twenty minutes." And she disappeared behind the door.

I stared at the blank paper for a long time.

It matched my mind, devoid of thoughts. Abruptly, I leaned into my nightstand, picked up my phone, and dialed a number.

As the seconds ticked, my heart shot to my throat, and a familiar beep rang through the earpiece. "This phone number is no longer in service. Please check the number and try again." The message was familiar. So I saved the contact.

I clumped to Heather, who glazed butter on salmon in the kitchen, and handed her the letter.

"So, may I read it?"

"Yes. There's nothing there if you ask me."

"It's a start." She winked. "You signed it as 'Queen Elizabeth.' " A smile permanently plastered on her face.

Shrugging her off, I asked, "Do you need help?"

She handed me the salmon tray. "Just take it to the dining table. We got the rest covered. Right, Dina and Olivia?"

They nodded in an unreal harmony as Olivia smiled so wide, I thought I was dreaming.

I trudged to the dining table, placed the salmon on it, and slumped on a chair.

The front door creaked shut, and footsteps entered the villa while Heather studied my letter. "Liz, do you remember more now?"

"No." I scooped a handful of almonds from the green, ceramic bowl in the center of the table by the salmon.

"Maybe you remember more than you are aware," a male voice said.

I paused munching and eyed him. After placing a bouquet of roses on the coffee table in the living room, he swaggered to me in his Hawaiian shirt and casual khaki shorts.

Dina and Olivia stopped rinsing plates at the sink to watch.

"Who are you?" I rose.

Heather joined us. "Adam, this is Liz, one of our girls, and Liz, this is—"

"One of her boys." He shook my hand with twinkles in his eyes.

Heather laughed and slapped his shoulder playfully. "You wish, Adam. Liz, he is my cousin."

He held his chest and squinted. "Ouch, that hurt, Hiwalani." Turning to me, he lowered. "Do I strike you as Heather's cousin?"

I gazed into his blue eyes. "You don't strike me as Hawaiian, at least."

"He isn't. He's related to me by law, not blood." Busying herself in moving the plates around on the dining table, she asked, "Adam, are you staying for dinner?"

Strangely, he scrutinized my face. Lamplight reflected on his light brown, long hair as his big, watery eyes peered into mine.

At least six feet two, he towered over me. He stroked his beard as I tore my gaze from him to Heather, who had gone to the kitchen and stared at the cutting board but chopped nothing.

I whispered, "Of course. You don't need my permission to stay."

"Hiwalani, I've been asked. I'll join you."

Heather nodded at Dina and Olivia, and they brought the rest of the bowls to the table. The aroma of lemon capers already laced my throat before Dina lifted the lid off the salad.

"Looks delicious," he mouthed and took the seat next to me.

My surroundings blurred while I focused on him wiping his beard and mouth with his napkin. He then spread it across his lap and removed its wrinkles meticulously. Contours of a built physique shaped his shirt as he met my gaze. "What's Liz short for?"

I turned my attention to my own napkin, hoping he didn't notice me staring. "What do you mean?" For unknown reasons, my cheeks burned.

"Are you a Leslie? An Elizabeth?"

Heather, Dina, and Olivia sat across from us.

"The second one."

"Like the queen?" He chuckled and so did Olivia.

"Named like her but not a queen." I tipped a salmon onto my plate and passed the bowl to him while Dina filled her plate with salad, sticking to her vegan diet.

After Adam served himself a piece, I wondered if Heather was setting him up with a cold, pregnant woman. Not a first! Still, he differed from the other men Heather had brought home out of the blue. He was happy, humorous, and comfortable. All silverware clinked, bringing my attention to how formal the dinner was today. Most nights, we filled our plates in the kitchen and brought to the table, and sometimes we didn't eat together at all.

"It's nice to meet you in person." He wiped his mouth with the napkin. "I've heard a lot about you."

"Really? That can't be good." I played with the salad on my plate.

"Why would you say that?" Again, the hint of a smirk on his face, the smile that came from the eyes instead of the lips: 'the Adam smile.'

"Never mind."

He tilted his head, scratched his beard, and spoke softly. "Do you remember nothing of your past, not an event, not a person?"

I shook my head and stared into space, recalling my dream about Desiree. Dina, Olivia, and Heather chewed on their food silently—a rarity in the carefully orchestrated meeting, one that disallowed my crude and untimely anger, I bet.

With each word, his gaze pierced through my soul. "You're the most unique person I've met. Most of us are told what to do: Go to college, find a job. But by choice or not, here you are."

I sighed. "I would trade triteness for my life any day of the year."

"And I refuse to trade today with any other day."

I tucked a lose strand of hair behind my ear under his watchful eye. My heart missed a distinct beat, and a word went missing in my mental vocabulary to describe the moment.

"I can help you find triteness in your tribulation." He put down his fork. "Do you know regular people also suffer from memory loss?"

"What're you trying to say?" I suppressed a giggle.

"Take old age, for instance. There are three signs of old age, and the first one is memory loss."

I snorted. "Are you saying I'm old?"

"Not at all. I'm getting old though, and I can prove it." He grinned.

"Okay . . ."

I waited for the punchline and waved my fork at him. "Prove it. What other two signs of old age?"

He shook his head, picking his fork. "I forget the other two signs!"

Everyone burst into laughter.

"See, I told you."

I smiled. "What do you do for a living, Adam?"

He rotated his fork in the air, staring at it. "Nowadays, I'm in the construction business. A builder, some would say." He sighed. "I build structures out of nothing, reconstruct broken pieces." He glanced at Heather before turning to me. "What do you do?" he asked, and I dropped my fork.

Heather lifted her head. "Liz started the newsletter in print and online, doubling our donations. More people know about our little organization for women."

"Damn impressive." He resumed eating.

"For a forgetful person, you mean?"

He chuckled. "It's impressive for an average person like me, but yeah, in your situation, only great mental strength could realize concrete success in such a short amount of time."

My cheeks warmed further.

"It does." Heather rose and marched to the sink with her empty plate. Olivia and Dina followed.

"Aren't you going to finish?" Adam smiled, and I returned his grin.

If he'd asked me out, I would have said yes right then and there.

In my new life of two months, no one had uttered "I love you" or kissed me even though I was with child.

After Adam bid me farewell the first night, another dimension opened in my life. My heart drummed like a ticking clock. A hunger brewed inside me. I listened to all phone rings awaiting his beaconing, studying all vehicles pulling into our driveway pining for his green pickup truck. On the third day, I leaped on the buzzing telephone. Adam.

His voice made me giggle like a schoolgirl. I couldn't recognize the person I had become, but it didn't matter because nothing surmounted the possibility of being wanted even if for a night.

"Want to dine with me tonight?" He went straight to the point, and a "yes" slipped out of my lips too fast. I couldn't care less that he sounded too polished for a construction worker or wonder why an amnesiac, pregnant woman would appeal to him.

He promised to pick me in an hour, and I ran to the bathroom, tugged at my cheeks to plump, and puckered my lips.

I slipped into Dina's tiny black dress that made me forget I had a round belly. Thankfully, it fit.

When the doorbell rang, my heart hammered inside my chest. I finished the final strokes of blush and waltzed to the door. Grateful to be alone at home, I was out of breath before I popped open the door.

He wore a collared sky-blue shirt and khaki pants. The topmost button was open, revealing a white vest, and instead of flowers or chocolates, he held handles of a bicycle. "Ready?"

I tilted my head. "A cycle?"

"Yes, we can bike along the coast."

"I thought . . ."

He yanked down the bike's stand with his foot and grabbed my hands. "Did I disappoint you?" His thumb caressed my palm. "I can return the rental."

"No, it's all right. I should probably change." I released my hands.

His eyes glimmered. "Why?"

I chuckled, holding my dress. "This will be a grave injustice to biking."

"You look nice in it. It'll be fine." His cheeks reddened as he split into his lovely Adam smile.

I grabbed my purse and locked the door before glancing around and asking, "Where's mine?"

"No, you can't be biking in your condition. I brought this extension for you." He patted a smaller second seat perched over a third wheel with separate pedals and handles. "Hop on."

I tucked a loose strand of hair behind my ear and slipped my purse across my shoulders. Holding my tiny but obvious twenty-week belly, I put one leg over the bike. When it wobbled, I latched onto his back, avoiding starting our first date with a fall.

"Are you okay?"

"Yes," I said, pulling down my knee-length dress.

I placed my legs on the pedals without letting go of his firm shoulders, and we headed north on the bike trail, the ocean lining our right. The breeze lifted my hair, and the palm trees rustled as I admired his muscular back inside his tight shirt, wondering what it would be like to slide my fingers against his contours.

My head dropped to his back, and I closed my eyes, relishing the breeze frisking my body.

Around a secluded bend, he pulled over, and I steadied myself against him while dismounting the bike. A group of teenagers played volleyball on the beach by the parking lot.

I brushed the creases off my black dress. "Where are we going?"

"You'll see."

He parked the bike at the designated racks and held my hand climbing uphill toward a restaurant perched at the summit.

We sat at a cozy table by the wall-to-wall windows, overlooking Kapaa's entire coastline.

Distracted by every little detail, even the steady breaths inside my throat, I couldn't focus on a syllable inside the menu. So I yanked it shut and folded my hands over. My foot tapped involuntarily, and I crossed my legs, pressing them down. "If you don't mind me asking, how much money do construction workers make?"

He chuckled, sipping his ice water. "Do you always go straight to the point?"

"I'm sorry for being rude. It's an age-old problem. Two months to be precise."

He laughed and opened his menu. "The view is priceless and so is our time together—both things money can't buy."

Tina Turner's song "What's Love Got to Do with It" played softly in the background.

I sat upright. "True. Listen, Adam, I want to tell you something. I'm not keeping—"

He shushed me and reached for my hands, squeezing them. "Let's talk about her later."

"Her?"

"Yes. Heather told me."

That loudmouth! She had dragged me to the ultrasound and inundated me with adoption paperwork when all I wanted was to continue uninterrupted with Adam and feel beautiful again. His caressing my hands was the only comfort in my present.

He had become the first sliver of excitement in my life for which I wanted to live here versus at an unknown place. I cleared my throat. "It's a girl, but I don't want her."

His face twitched. "Why not?"

"Is it important?" I freed my hands and reached for the locket on my gold chain, the only remnant from my past life besides the creature inside me.

He crossed his arms. "What if you wanted the baby before losing your memory?"

"I doubt it, and besides . . ." I glanced around, wallowing deeply. Wealthy people dined here. Not me. "I want to start fresh," I admitted. "I want nothing to do with my past, especially because she is as unwanted as I am."

He coughed on his water and cleared his throat. "Why would you think the baby and you are unwanted?"

Why did he care so much about my child, the baby I had scheduled to abort in a week?

The server arrived and wrote down our order. And I excused myself to use the restroom right after. When I returned, our food had arrived, and we exchanged awkward smiles, busying ourselves with our salads.

The sun descended along with our dinner, and afterward, we returned the bike rental a mile away and strolled to the villa.

Nothing could quieten the ocean's waves that had become second nature to me. But after two memorable months on the island, they still drew me in as if I was a tourist from the mainland, their roar captivating.

He laced his fingers with mine, rubbing his thumb against my palm. "Do you remember anything from your past?"

"No."

"Do you have no hunch about the father?"

"None. I know nothing about my family or . . ."

"Or?"

"I remember a friend named Desiree."

He halted. "What do you remember?"

"I dream about her almost daily. She appears the same every time with the same face and clothes: corduroy pants and a red pleated shirt." I cleared my throat. "Sometimes we're happy, enjoying each other's company, but most of the time, it's a nightmare in which one of us is dying."

He didn't blink, and his surety was intimidating.

"You don't question my dreams?"

"No. Rather, I can help you find her."

He leaned in, his breath warming my face, and I shivered. Before I could turn away, he stooped and pressed his lips against mine. His mustache tickled my chin, and my heart galloped.

A barking dog on a leash strolled around the corner, its owner leading him past us down the trail as we broke apart and resumed our stroll.

I touched my lips with my hand and whispered, "I don't even know her last name."

"Oh, it's a small world."

Cars swished past us on one side, and the ocean waves splashed on the other. "What are you going to do?"

"Do you believe in destiny?"

We stopped to look into each other's eyes again, his face serious.

"I—"

He placed his hand softly on my lips. "Do you trust me?"

I couldn't tear myself from the depth of his blue eyes and nodded, his fingers still rubbing against my lips as he cradled me into his arms, pressed against my body, and kissed me hard. I laced my fingers against his hair, savoring the best minute of my life.

We slowly pulled apart as he tucked my hair behind my ear, and I reached for his hand, leading him home. A faint smile formed on his face as I rested my head on his shoulders the rest of the walk.

Although I tugged on his hand, signaling my willingness to take the next step at the door, he kissed me with a promise of daily walks along the coast, said goodbye, and left. My days brightened in an instant, and imaginary fireworks lit the skies. I leaned against the door with my eyes closed, relishing his goodbye kiss before waltzing into my room. Changing into my nightclothes turned into a love song recital.

I sat by my window, humming and watching the moonlit ocean. My dreams formed like clouds, floating like the palm trees, and I never bothered to ask him about his past, nor would I in the days that followed. I fondly considered us first-time lovers, never loved before, never tainted. Like no one else existed.

Life was good.

The Good Life

*The Benches along the Kapaa Bike Trail
Four Days Later*

FIVE WALKS, TWO LUAUS, and uncountable kisses later, Adam didn't show for our morning walk. Tapping my foot, I waited for him on a bench along the Kapaa bike trail. It'd already been an hour, and the sun burnished high in the sky.

I sighed and rose, pacing the area. Two texts sent, and no replies. Heather didn't know his whereabouts either. Wouldn't he have canceled if he couldn't make it? I hung my head and breathed. There was Adam. And his smile. Both inseparable—now both gone. Swallowing my pride, I trudged to the villa alone. He didn't return my messages or turn on his phone.

The next day, I called him at the crack of dawn. Nothing.

I was a fool to expect love at my lowest point in life.

I brushed my teeth, cursing at my puffy eyes. "Fool!" I yelled, glaring into the mirror.

I rinsed my mouth and touched my newly formed double chin, even my face became unacceptable in pregnancy. I stormed out of there. In my gym shoes and fleece, I stared at the front door, waiting. Nothing.

So, I walked alone, searching for him, the wind tousling my hair.

I typed him a sappy text message on the way home, tears dripping from my face. How had I turned into a stalker? I cringed and hit backspace before dialing the abortion clinic instead.

Such a large lump formed in my throat, I thought I would bawl when the time came to say hello. My thoughts became darker and didn't stop at the murder of a baby.

They wanted me gone.

Someone on the other end answered, and I rescheduled my appointment from two days later to that very afternoon.

Afterall, what use were days when the minutes within were empty? With Adam gone and Heather away to meet her new boyfriend, Dudley, for the day, it was my chance.

I showered, and my gut gurgled, reeling under a hurricane inside my body.

An hour later when the construction drilling had peaked, I toddled toward the front door, and my foot hit the dresser where we tossed our keys on our way into the villa. I groaned as my heartache became physical. A drawer had opened from the collision, and a bag kept me from shoving it shut. With my gaze glued on its floral print, I scooped it with trembling fingers as though I stole royal secrets.

I slumped into the plush seat next to the drawer and scanned the villa, empty like my life. The bag contained already-opened, numbered envelopes, and I pulled out a letter from the first one.

The shelter's phone rang, and I jumped, scattering the envelopes and the letter on the floor.

I silenced the call because this wasn't the time to play a secretary for Heather and then picked the envelopes carefully, dusting off the letter tainted by the ground.

A glance at my watch warned me only a half hour separated me from my appointment, and I read the letter with renewed urgency.

August 9, 2013

Dear Jason,

I can still feel the touch of your fingers against my skin and hear the babbling fountain in the atrium over our lengthy conversations on life, love, and writing. Our laughter tears through my brain.

The writers' conference is over now. So is our intimate love affair. I drift from anger to a weak, disgusting longing of embracing you one more time. Who am I fooling? I wish I could hold you a thousand more times.

I put the letter face down in my lap. My mind battled my heart if I should go on. The construction drills had stopped, amplifying the deafening silence. My heart ached. Somewhere, a tap dripped rhythmically, as though alarming for a dam explosion. I picked the letter again.

I need time to tire of you as you and Isabella grew weary of each other, or perhaps you have rekindled your marriage. Perhaps you two are happier than you showed. Why did you move on so quickly? Was I that forgettable?

Forever yours,
Queen Elizabeth

The letter fell to the floor. I clutched my chest. Elizabeth. Me. Son of a gun!

My breaths became cold, and my hands quivered.

A tear seeped out, and Heather's words rang in my ears: "I know your name and age from a note I found on you, but I've misplaced it."

I called the clinic. "I'm sorry, but I'm unable to make it today. Is the time for Wednesday still available?" It was.

After the call ended, I shoved the contents of the first letter into its envelope. Rattling keys on the front door ticked like an automated bomb seconds from an explosion. I stuffed the envelopes inside the bag, shuffled to my room, and slammed the door shut as someone entered the villa. Placing the letters in my cupboard, I locked it and stepped back.

It was the first time I'd used the lock. I'd never had a reason to hide anything before, my life as empty as a dried-up basin.

The footfalls loudened.

I hid the key in my purse and clasped my mouth. Heather and I were different in one regard. I locked my secrets, and she stashed them in an accessible drawer. The knock that followed almost toppled me to the floor. I took a deep breath and opened the door with an ear-to-ear grin.

Dina wore a blazer over her jeans and a collared shirt, her shoulder-length brown hair tied back in a small ponytail. "Do I look like an executive?"

I nodded. "Sure. Where are you going?"

"Not me, us—to the retirement home. Did you forget?" She touched my shoulder. "You look pale. Are you okay?"

I scratched the back of my head. "Yes. I forgot. Let's go." I grabbed my purse under her steady gaze, sure that Dina had rescued me from the rest of the letters, the clinic, and myself . . . but not forever.

Night fell, and Heather returned from Honolulu.

Sipping my soup at the dinner table, I stared at her wondering what else she had hidden from me. My foot erupted in a constant tap.

I ached to read the letters, but Dina had kept me busy all day. The first to finish dinner, I hurriedly excused myself and rushed to my baby pink bedroom.

I ripped a sheet off the notepad from my nightstand and wrote the facts from my letters, starting with Jason.

In barged Dina, and I crumpled the paper into a ball. "Dina, don't you knock?"

"I'm sorry, but we've got work to do. Don't go to sleep yet."

"Exposing the retirement home?"

"Yes."

I titled my head. "Can we do it tomorrow?"

Dina slumped on the bed. "You saw how bad they . . ." Her eyes lowered and widened before she swept her hand against my wet cheek. "You're crying, my God! What happened?"

I stared at my hands and whispered, "Adam's gone. He left me."

"He left you?" Her eyes widened.

"Yes. He missed our daily walks. Twice. I haven't seen him for two days."

She flung her hands in the air and jumped on the bed. "Only two days? Oh, come on, give the man little space. I'm sure he must have a good reason."

"I have a bad feeling about it. He didn't tell me—"

The door flung open again, and Heather marched inside the room.

"*Gees*, no one in this house knocks!" I jerked my head.

Dina sat upright. "Heather, do you know where Adam is?"

"I haven't been able to contact him. He must be on a remote island for business, but don't worry, Liz. He'll be back." She tilted her head forward and narrowed her eyes. "Are you crying?" She shook her head. "Let me call this man." And she stormed out of the room, the wood creaking under her bulky frame.

I wiped my tears, fetched my laptop from the nightstand, and opened its lid before Dina grasped my arm. "Are you sure you're okay to continue?"

"Yes, you are right what we saw today at the retirement home needs attention."

By midnight, we published the article. Dina was content with our prompt action, but only Adam and his lack of a goodbye lingered in my heart. All departures should end in a farewell greeting. Why hadn't ours?

CHAPTER 5 - THE IMPROPER GOODBYE

"To all the pretty and gloomy places, I treaded away from without knowing I was leaving forever; I wish to see you one more time. So I can steeple my hands, bow my head, and acknowledge we are parting ways. Have a ceremony of sorts. Forgive the misgiving and rejoice the happiness."
Mars D. Gill

The Last Day

The Gaylord Hotel, Orlando, FL
August 9, 2013

ANNA TRUDGED OUT OF HER ROOM like a fifteen-year-old girl on an exam day. Her face glowed even though her steps shivered, exposing her fear.

The crowd had lessened, and people from their teams, including Sue, had flown out that morning to beat the tropical storm now pounding Orlando.

Jason and Anna had spent last night in each other's embrace, sharing childhood memories. His touch and his dimpled smile had etched itself onto her spirit.

Afterward, they sat in his rented car and made their way to the airport in silence. Now and then, they exchanged nervous smiles. The unutterable jargon of emotions danced in their eyes through wistful glances.

"What will happen when we land in Chicago?" she asked as relentless rain pounded on the car.

He let out a big sigh. "We'll figure something out."

"I'll be your Mrs. on the side?"

"In shady, dingy motel rooms." He half-smiled with a furrowed brow as Anna elbowed him.

He erupted into a full-blown laughter. "I know, Ms. Everly, you don't believe in destiny. I do."

"And?"

"Everything will fall in place."

She shook her head. "Dingy hotels aren't for me."

"I know. You belong in a castle, celebrated like a queen."

She chuckled before brooding silence took over, engulfing the words unspoken.

The rain ceased as soon as they reached the airport. Both of their flights were on time, despite the storm canceling several. They checked in and marched to the security line leading to Anna's departure gate. Jason leaned in and squeezed her hand. "I'll see you in Chicago. Wait at your gate, okay?" He left her with a peck on the cheek as she nodded through a film of tears, teetering behind the row of heads.

When she reached the conveyer belt, she jerked her purse over her head, but it got caught around her neck. Struggling and releasing it, she threw it on the belt, imagining her apartment in Lincoln Park. Biting her lip and staring at her feet, she held her neck. What was once a comfortable haven, her home, now sent lonely shivers down her spine. She shuddered through the x-ray screen, anticipating a long, dreary heartbreak. Would the TSA discover her sorrow?

During the flight, too, grief suspended in the air as passengers glared at Anna for sighing loudly. She stared out the window but didn't take in the scenery. The armrests alone kept her intact, preventing her from melting away in her agony.

At Chicago, the seatbelt sign beeped. She jittered. With her heart pounding, her insides wept, bleeding gallons of anxiety. She followed the slow-moving heads out of the plane. Outside, she wrung her hands, craning her neck around the crowd with a parched throat. Had her last meeting with him passed?

Jason Barnes was nowhere.

CHAPTER 6 – THE VOID OF A GOODBYE

"The hole of a farewell I fill with new jewels of silence, tears, and mercy."
Mars D. Gill

Still Without a Farewell

Hawaii
Five Months Later

I GLARED AT THE UNUSED CEILING FAN in my bedroom. Loaded with dust, it hung over me like a black cloud. My elbow rubbed against Dina's as the damp floral bedsheet beneath me clung to my back, and a chick chirped outside my window. Its song might have been happy, but my ears only registered its groans. The clock's ticks and a distant car's swish grated against my ears.

Seeking comfort in Dina's gentle snores, I held a pillow to my head and shut my eyes. I thought about Jason while waiting for Adam.

Where was our goodbye? How I longed to text Adam one more time.

But I refused to let my desperation win.

My cell rang, and I fetched it from my nightstand before it almost slipped beneath my fingers while Dina rolled over and sighed. I trembled, tiptoeing to the attached bathroom.

Seven in the morning. An unknown number.

"Hello?" I whispered, gently shutting the door behind me.

"Can I speak with Elizabeth? L-Liz?" a coarse female voice boomed.

"Speaking. Who's this?" I bolted the bathroom door.

"They're lying to you."

I froze and clutched my chest. "What? Who's lying to me?"

"Heather—"

"Do you know me from my past life?" I leaned against the bathroom door and shut my eyes.

She breathed heavily.

I scratched my head, pacing the tiny bathroom. "Who are you?"

"Who I am isn't important. Trust me, all of them are lying to you. Heather, Adam—"

"No!"

"I have to go!"

"Wait! Hello? Hello!" I stared at my phone, but she had gone.

I shut the toilet seat and slumped on it, holding my phone against my lips while shaking. Was my life not complicated enough?

Heather lied to me. But Adam? A chill crept up my spine. I rose.

I lived in a safe house for women, for God's sake, and Heather, the warmest person in my life, had betrayed me. However, I had no qualms about fending for myself. I ripped a long piece off the toilet roll and searched the cupboard. I stashed pens everywhere, and sure enough, I found a pencil.

I sat down and wrote. Writer. Conference. Jason and the wife, Isabella. August 2013. I counted the months on my fingers. Five. Math checked out too—Jason had to be the father. Maybe I used to be a queen. A steamy affair and quick abandonment . . . made sense.

A knock thumped on the bathroom door, and I jumped.

"Liz, are you okay?" Dina asked.

All of them are lying to you. Was Dina in on it?

"Why do you ask?"

"Please—"

"Are you hiding anything from me?" I crumpled the paper.

"No." She knocked. "Open the door. Why would you ask that question?"

"Heather is lying to me, and I'm not opening the door." I sat upright.

"What are you talking about?" Dina banged once on the door, sighing.

"I don't know," I whispered.

A moment's silence passed, and she whispered, "Open the door and talk to Heather."

I rose and placed my hand against the cold wood. "If you say a word to Heather, we are no longer sisters."

"But—"

"Dina!"

She sighed. "Heather loves you like a daughter. Whenever you're ready, talk to her, okay? I promise I won't say a word to her."

Dina's footsteps receded.

The clandestine letters and the cursed phone call tarnished Heather forever.

How could I trust her now?

After Dina shut the outside door, I marched out into my pink bedroom and pulled the letters out of the cupboard, unfolding the second letter so fast the paper almost ripped.

August 15, 2013

Dear Jason,

Sue returned from her extended vacation today, and her face reminded me of the five days we spent together, but I didn't need the reminder. Why can't I move on with my life?

Ironically, the men whose hearts I had broken have settled down with steady, well-paying jobs and large families. How did I find this little information? I got desperate and called them.

I am truly and blissfully alone, but I have an unwanted companion no one can see—you, your face, your dimples, your kiss.

How do I exorcise you?

Your queen,

Elizabeth

The letters contained Morse codes into my past life. I unfolded the crumpled toilet paper and wrote the name Sue, bolding it. While tracing Jason and Isabella's names, the paper tore. The ghosts of my past knocked on my door through the letters.

But while an endless abyss of memory loss trapped me, where were Jason and Isabella?

Jason and Isabella

Chicago
September 2013

JASON GUZZLED a glass of water in one big swoop as the jazz musicians blended into black shadows against the orange shimmers of Lake Michigan. He cleared his throat and wiped the sweat off his brow, rethinking the sweater-vest he wore. Yellow and orange leaves drifted to the ground around the open-walled restaurant. He too had been shedding old habits.

While Isabella buried her face in a menu, Jason focused on the live, soft music as a waiter walked in their direction.

"What would you like to drink?" the waiter asked.

Isabella ordered a Mango Martini.

"Can I have another one of these?" Jason shook his empty water cup. Only ice clinked against its sides.

"Certainly."

"Why? Are you not going to order your Blue Moon?" Isabella's eyebrow arched.

"Not today."

Her stare lingered before returning to the menu. She huddled under the cool outdoor breeze as Jason tugged his sweater-vest lower. A couple held hands on the table next to theirs. An older pair danced near the musicians.

Three generations of a family sat at the end of the row, ranging from infants to grandparents. The restaurant staff sang a birthday song at their table. Their own children were away at his in-laws' home. It was date night.

Well, it was supposed to be.

"We need to talk." Jason lifted his water glass to sip, but it was empty.

Isabella put the menu down and folded her hands over it. "Let's order first."

"We need to talk." He coughed into his fist, his eyes watering, his throat constricting.

She reached for his hands. "What's wrong, honey?"

"I've been meaning to talk to you for a month now."

"Your behavior hasn't gone unnoticed." A smirk widened on her face. "Ever since your 'writers' conference' from a month ago, you aren't yourself. God, you haven't touched me." A sarcastic chuckle slipped out of her mouth with a razor-sharp focus on Jason. "You can't sleep, and when you're up, the bed gets heavy— three times its weight." She shook her head and opened her menu. "Let's talk after we order. Okay?"

Jason's cheek twitched, forcing a smile, but only one side cooperated. "I need to—"

The waiter returned and refilled Jason's glass with water.

Isabella smiled. "We're ready to order. I'll have the shrimp Cobb salad, and he'll have the lobster ravioli. The usual." She handed her menu to him.

As soon as the waiter left, she rose, grabbed his hands, and pulled him to an upright position.

"What're you doing? I've been trying—"

"After we dance." She dragged him onto the dance floor as if he was an unwilling toddler. Her fitted black dress plunged into a low neckline, accentuating her figure, like always, dressed to kill.

She pressed on his hands and swayed, encouraging him to do the same. But Jason continued to resist, a storm raging inside his body. Sighing, he pushed Isabella away.

To his surprise, she flew back and fell, her legs flung apart revealing her lace underwear. Gasps rose in the restaurant. Although the musicians didn't stop playing, they went offbeat for a second.

"Shoot!" Jason covered his mouth under the glare of an old lady who had risen with fury. He helped Isabella stand, whispering, "I'm so sorry, babe. If only you would listen to me."

The Isabella he knew would have slapped him on the face. The one standing in front of him tucked a loose strand of hair behind her hair, her cheeks red.

She giggled and said to their onlookers, "Oh, if you think that was violent, you should see us in our bedroom at midnight!"

A few people laughed, but the old lady, who now stood akimbo, glared at Jason. Isabella pushed his extended hand away as she marched to their table, where the waiter laid their food. "Bon appétit," he said before waltzing away.

Isabella and Jason glowered at each other, still not seated.

"I believe you are in a hurry to tell me you don't love me anymore." She lifted her chin.

He stiffened.

"Sit! Our food is getting cold." She plunged into her seat, sprinkling black pepper on her salad.

Jason stared at her but obeyed. "I met someone at the conference," he whispered.

Isabella cut into her salad like it was a well-cooked filet mignon. The white plate under the rich kale took the brunt of her knife's fury, screeching and scratching.

"I—"

"Shush!" Isabella yelled. She raised her hand, and the waiter rushed toward them.

"This is stale," she said, rolling her knife over the salad.

The waiter's cheeks reddened before he drowned Isabella in an ocean of apology.

"I like my kale crisp and fresh. You brought me soggy Scottish summer!"

He whisked the salad away with a promise of crisp kale on a new one.

"Jason, my innocent love. Am I stupid?" she shouted in a whisper.

He stared at her without flinching. "No."

"But I am." Her eyes widened. "I gave up my career after Andrew's birth and slogged—to keep the house clean and take care of the kids, feeding them, bathing them, and making them do their homework. I was loyal to you every second of the day. I. Am. Stupid." She slammed her napkin on the table while Jason curled his fingers into a fist before folding his hands tight on the table.

He clenched his teeth. "I never asked you to give up your career. Rather, I've always wanted you to pursue your goals. Staying at home—"

"Made me an ignorant housewife?"

"No!" He clenched his teeth. "But you know how our conversations changed."

Isabella laughed and rose from her seat, marching toward the musicians before Jason shot up in his chair with his mouth open. "Where are you going?"

She found an unused microphone in front of the jazz musicians, who were on a break, while Jason clutched his face, slumping into his chair as the microphone screeched.

"My husband waltzes off to fancy conferences and makes out with women." Isabella pointed at Jason. "Cheater!"

The pianist behind her chuckled.

"I mean, look at my ass. It's tight as it was in high school. So what if I stay at home? I rock it, baby!"

When a staff member marched toward Isabella, she left the stage and headed toward the exit, swiping at her cheeks.

Jason sat in his chair, his hands covering his face. Stilted laughter and hushed whispers infiltrated the space, but they were nothing compared to the piercing glare from the old lady who had again risen and stood ten feet from him.

He slammed his napkin on the table, left cash for the food, and followed Isabella.

Outside, stars now dotted the sky, and the lake shimmered as though with his tears. He wiggled on his coat, spotting Isabella's frame.

She sat on a concrete rock along the shore.

In hushed whispers, she rambled into her phone. Jason stopped in his tracks.

She hadn't ever mentioned having any friends in the decade he had known her. Strange but true. She claimed women were jealous of her obvious beauty.

So who was she talking to?

She turned and spotted him, then hung up, and clambered to her feet, fixing her hair. "Let's go."

"Who were you talking to?"

Her eyes glittered. "It doesn't matter." She slid her arm in his and pulled him. "Shall we?"

"Go where?"

"Home. Where else?"

Home

Chicago
November 2013

"HOME," she'd said.

Home had become fifty sleepless nights, trapped in the city that added one hundred crime-related deaths to its tainted record. On the fifty-first day, Jason rode in the Metra to the city. People cradling cigarettes swaggered off the commuter train along with him to the green building housing the *ChicagoGoers* magazine. He was done living half a life, ready to fight for Anna.

But when he arrived, Sue delivered an uncomfortable truth: Anna's work performance had fallen, starting from the Orlando conference, forcing her to take a leave of absence.

He scoured his phone for minutes. However, neither her coworkers nor the vast array of social media held answers. All traces of Anna had vanished.

Twenty minutes later, he hopped on the Metra back to his suburban home, wounded and battered. When he entered through his front door, he expected an empty house. After all, regardless of what she'd said, surely Isabella would have packed her things and taken off with the kids, leaving him to suffer alone.

He'd harbored the same suspicion for months. But just as before, his intuition proved wrong.

His entire family sat in the dining room. The kids spread their notebooks on the table as Isabella guided them with their homework. She forced a smile, and Josh, the littlest, ran to him. Jason was relieved and yet unable to find comfort as though numb to his heart's core.

After dinner, Jason tucked the children in bed and read them their favorite stories. Once the home quieted, Isabella and Jason changed into their nightclothes in their bathroom.

"So, do you still see her?" She asked through the mirror while tying her hair back.

"Who?" He slipped on his shirt.

"The woman you had an affair with at the conference, of course." She grabbed her toothbrush, squished toothpaste on, and brushed rapidly.

"No." He turned on the water faucet to wash his hands.

"So, it's over?" she asked with a mouthful of suds.

Reluctant to admit his feelings, Jason dried his hands with a towel. "I don't have a way to contact her."

Isabella laughed as though he had cracked a joke. "So, if you did, would you contact her?"

Jason creased his brow, his wrinkles deepening on his forehead.

Isabella flung her toothbrush into its holder without rinsing it off and glared at him. "What do you want from me?"

"Leave me. I'm that worthless." He stroked his forehead. His inner voice called him a father's son, and he cringed lifting his gaze from his feet.

Isabella shook her head, holding it firmly with her hands. "I'm going nuts. At this rate, you'll find me in a mental asylum like your mother."

"Babe—"

She clenched her fist and punched the air. Her face crumpled, darkening ten shades, and tears sprung out like an overanimated emoji.

He dashed over and embraced her in his arms. "I'm so sorry, babe. Please don't cry. I promise we'll work something out."

His sarcastic, inner voice hissed again: A father's son. Jason shut his eyes.

He held her for several minutes, and she clung to him on the cold floor. Lifting her off the ground, he carried her to the bed and kissed her forehead. Her grasp on his back firmed, and she crushed her lips against his.

At first, he fought her tugs, but he couldn't stand seeing her weak. He relented, allowing her to take off his clothes, rub her hands against his back, kissing his neck until he was inside her, responding to her moaning with a heavy silence. The make-up sex had the opposite effect on each of them.

Afterward, Isabella slept peacefully beside him.

Not Jason.

He clenched his heavy heart, took short breaths, and cringed into his body. The guilt of having sex with the wife he wanted to leave kept him awake as he stared at the dark ceiling.

Mental asylum, she had said. He pinched his eyes shut.

"It's the right thing to do," his counselor had said.

In response, Jason had stared at his mother's face with flared nostrils. How could she agree to go to a mental asylum? She was the sanest person he knew who was hurting for good reasons. He followed her outside the home where the nurse led her to a car.

But she never looked at him when she slid inside a black sedan like a convicted felon. He pushed to get to his mom, but the nurse held him back. When the door shut, he banged on her car window, and the black sedan slipped away. He dashed after it until his legs gave way. Why didn't she look him in the eye once?

Isabella's snore thrust him into the present. He sighed, and her head popped up, but she didn't open her eyes. Shushing her, he carefully freed his grasp and put on his clothes.

He then tiptoed out of the room and down the stairs, stepping out into the moonlight and breathing in the fresh and frigid air.

If someone peeked inside his tough exterior, within those blue eyes, they'd find a helpless boy searching for love. He worried about Anna. Was she okay? Had he hurt the very person he loved? He paced on his patio.

When he returned to his bedroom, it was past three in the morning. And to his shock, the bed was empty, only crumpled wrinkles contoured their comforter.

He searched room to room and found her car in the garage but not Isabella. He preemptively dialed 9-1-1 before realizing he hadn't checked one last place. He rushed to their bedroom and flung open the closet.

Isabella sat on the floor, her tears splattering onto a stash of papers in her hands.

CHAPTER 7 - LETTERS FROM THE QUEEN

*"By the time you read this letter, these words will be those
of the past. The me of now is gone."*
Fennel Hudson, A Writer's Year - Fennel's Journal - No. 3

The Morse Codes in Letters

The Shelter, Hawaii
January 2014

MY LIFE ROLLED, one letter at a time.

August 16, 2013
Dear Jason,
A week ago, I opened my apartment's dreaded door, and the energy sucked out of my soul. Deathly darkness! Deafening silence. Suffocating air. I cringed, and my bags fell to the floor. I shoved them inside with my feet, shut the door, and marched outside, ambling under the yellow streetlights until my feet brought me to the grocery store around the corner.

My fridge was as devoid of food as my house was of love. But I didn't buy dinner. I grabbed three bottles of Merlot and opened one right in the store using the metal counter's edge. Taking a giant swig, I belittled a young worker and paid my dues.

By the time I'd left, bottle number one had been sucked dry. I smashed it on the sidewalk.

I'd become someone I couldn't recognize. Once at home, I cranked up the music and opened what I call "the world's best stationery." It's my lifesaving stash of writing pads, envelopes, and pens. So I wrote my first letter to you, my love, my pain. Words streamed out like tears.

I don't know why I started it. To forget you. Teach you a lesson. Perhaps both. Not everyone gets letters from the **queen**. But the blasted letters aren't helping me.

I worry my coworkers, who say I've changed, that I smile and talk less. They're right. I'm unfit to make my own decisions. The other day I found myself sitting on a street bench, lost. I'd forgotten where I was going—maybe an early onset of Alzheimer's.

On another note, **Sue** has gotten crazier. Although she's attracted to me, she set me up on a blind date with a guy. Juan. Perhaps she's telling me I'm single and my possibilities are endless.

I'm getting used to writing these. Forget about a closure. A letter gives me a pause after which all the usual symptoms return: heart pounding, sinking feeling, blood pressure rising. When will your void fill?

The queen (Who else?)

August 20, 2013
Dear Jason,
You'll be happy to know Juan charmed me with confidence, and I am not the least bit interested in him. He has too many cats. Things progressed so fast with you, and look where we landed. Slow is prudent, but I am unsure when I will meet him again; we didn't exchange numbers.
Can I confess on paper? I called **Purple Ink** and asked for you with full intention to listen to your voice but say nothing in response. Thankfully, you didn't answer, and I need not face your happiness without me.
I have **no friends or family**. People at work are worried about my strange aloofness, as they call it. They are concerned I may get fired, not for adultery but incompetence.
Never yours,
Only a king's queen

September 1, 2013
Dear Jason,
I haven't been able to write to you in two weeks. The flu found me. You picked up your phone last time I called.

I sensed the happiness in your voice. So I hung up without saying a word.

How did I become a stalker?

If I listened to the evil witch inside my head, I'd mail these letters to Isabella from Brazil. And **no one would ever know they were from me.** I should do that!

You deserve punishment for not fighting for me.

Oh. I just entered the "anger" phase. Time to toast!

Angry Queen Elizabeth

September 6, 2013

Dear Jason,

Here is a toast to our one-month UNION.

Sue—imagine Crazy Sue—thinks I'm going crazy. She pulled me aside and called me out on it, and I told her the truth about us. On her insistence, I turned in a written request for an extended time off—probation of sorts. And guess what? They accepted it.

I didn't even need an excuse, like a death in the family or childbirth or a wedding. My manager simply said, "I'm glad you asked. You seem to be struggling lately." In other words, I was undergoing a life altering event. Can you call heartbreak that?

Thanks to my years of service, they let me take six months off without losing my job. Without pay though, of course.

Six months of free time. What should I do? I should check in to a rehab facility to revitalize my spirit, discover myself, and lose you. Why don't you ever come to me?

My anger has fled. I must retrace my steps.

The wretched queen

October 1, 2013

Dear Jason,

I am at a place where time stands still. It sings in Hawaii's acoustic waves, burns in the tiki torches' glow, and swings with Kauai's women's hula; oh, their elegant moves and smiles. The wrinkly, green, towering mountains rule this land. And even though it will be two months since we last met, I'm okay because the time has come to a halt. Some exceptional hours breathe in my day when I can willfully enjoy my life. And not throw every second of every minute down the toilet.

And yet, here I am, writing to you again.

I will be **thirty-six years old** tomorrow.

Do you think about me?

I'm unsure how long I'll write these, as my questions keep my heartbreak chapter open forever. No closure in view.
The Hawaiian queen

October 2, 2013
My love,
I forgive you.
Today is my **birthday**.
I am losing the years of my life, but that is trivial when surviving each day is hard enough.
I've been sitting at the **Kōke'e State Park's** summit for hours. Beneath me is a green valley studded by sharp-edged, wrinkly mountains on either side. Myriads of soft clouds float in and out.
One second, I am shrouded by a white garb of wet clouds, and the next, they float away, revealing a bright-blue ocean beyond the valley. Far away in the middle of the ocean is an umbrella of clouds in the otherwise blue sky, where it is raining, and in the middle of the cloud patch is a spectacular rainbow. I feel God painted my life in it. In the hours I invested here, I let the clouds paint scene after scene. I shed a few tears—the happy kind—and took a hundred family photos of fellow tourists to fill their frames.

But above all, I thought about you. I wish I could have shared the experience with you. It would have made you happy.

My health is poor lately. I need to get back to a healthy diet and not eat like a tourist all the time. From now on, no more lovesick ice cream, just healthy Hawaiian pineapples.

I miss you so much, I could cry right here, right now in front of all these people.

God, I pray to forget you each passing day. But since it's my birthday, I take a solemn oath. I will be myself again. Accomplished. Driven. Happy.

Still your queen, believe it or not.

I rocked in my chair with my eyes closed. The creaks soothed my chaotic mind.

Had I stalked Jason? I'd called his office . . . now Adam vanished like him.

I pulled out my phone from my jean's pocket.

I had called Adam dozens of times in the preceding days.

Oh, dear God. I was a stalker!

I leaned forward, covering my mouth. Had Jason taken care of me and my uncontrollable mind?

I slumped back in my chair, and my belly grumbled. I'd finished reading the letters, and they held no more clues. While putting them back in the bag, a paper in the outside pocket brushed against my fingers.

I hadn't noticed it before. Quickly, I opened the flap, and out came a small but sealed envelope. Untampered. The people who'd read my letters hadn't gotten to this.

I hurriedly tore the seal and unfolded the note, too small to be called a letter:

These belong to you.
Your well-wisher,
S.

CHAPTER 8 - SUE MILLER

"Positive words left unsaid are like sachets of currency notes burnt in vain. Positive deeds left undone are like deep wells filled with soil to the brim. Do the undone, say the unsaid and turn the unturned."
Israelmore Ayivor

Sue's End of Conference

Chicago
August 9, 2013

SUE DEPLANED from the first flight in Chicago and drove to Highland Park, taking the Deerfield Road exit toward the lake.

As beautifully described by David, she drove past the Metra lines, where tall trees studded each side of the road. Towering mansions paved the path to her destination: the red brick building hidden behind pine trees and a giant metallic gate.

What a grand house! No one could guess trouble lived behind its elegant doors.

She pulled up to the contraption and pressed a button. It buzzed, and when the gate slid open, Sue's heart raced, rounding into a porch resembling a hotel lobby.

With arms folded, a woman stood holding the front door open with her back. Sue tilted her head and narrowed her eyes, trying to measure up the woman, who was neither dark nor light, neither fat nor slim. Sue licked her lips and got out of the car. Dark brown curls framed her elegant features.

"Who are you?" She tightened her arms across her chest.

Sue extended her arm. "Are you Jason Barnes's wife?"

"Yes, but he's not here." She shook Sue's hand but quickly released it.

"I know. I came here to talk to you. My name is Sue Miller, and I'm a writer with the *ChicagoGoers* magazine."

"Isabella Barnes."

"Do you have a few minutes?"

She hesitated before taking a step back. "Come in."

Isabella led her past a wall of photos exuding warm, loving memories.

Sue stopped in front of one as her jaw dropped. Why would someone thwart such a sanctuary of love?

Isabella turned. "Are you okay?"

Sue cleared her throat and rubbed her chest. "Yes, sorry. Beautiful home."

Expressionless, Isabella led her into the adjoining room, where all decorations were impersonal.

When Isabella offered a glass of cold water, Sue's feet trembled. She pressed one on top of another to stop the shaking before taking the glass from Isabella. "Thank you."

Isabella sat across from Sue and folded her arms. "Can we hurry? My baby will wake at any moment."

"How old is your baby?"

"He turned one in July."

Sue split into a nervous laugh. While sipping her water, she dribbled some down her shirt.

Her cheeks burning, she wiped her shirt and set the empty glass on the table between them. She cleared her throat. "It's a little out of place. But I wanted to talk to you about your husband. I just attended the East Coast Writers Conference with Jason. I consider it my duty to tell you—"

"What?" Isabella unfolded her arms and crossed her legs, pressing her lips together.

"He spent one-on-one time with an attractive woman at odd hours—a lot of time. I'll not give you her name, as she is my friend. I just want to inform you, and I hope you still have time to salvage your marriage."

Isabella's face reddened as though Sue had slapped her, and her hands limped for a second before curling into a fist. She spoke through clenched teeth. "What's your name again?"

Sue's face matched Isabella's ruddiness. "I'm Sue Miller." She handed her business card to Isabella. "I'm ready to help you in any way, shape, or form. The woman in question works with me. I could monitor her—"

"That'll be unnecessary. I trust my husband. If you're done, please leave now." Isabella lifted her chin and stood, gesturing to the door.

Sue sighed and stood. "As you wish." After following the hall to the door and stepping outside, she turned. "It's a lovely view of the lake from—"

Isabella slammed the door shut.

Sue's phone beeped. Her online date. She smiled. Perhaps she, too, could move on with her life. Taking charge was her second nature. But guilt toyed with her heart, and she worried. What if her efforts didn't pay off? What if Anna retaliated against her now that she'd turned Sue down?

Convinced of the nobility of her cause, Sue returned to work on Wednesday with a new purpose: get over Anna and start afresh. She avoided Anna all day, relieved no meetings were on schedule.

But why were there no meetings? The thought bothered the heck out of Sue.

At five o'clock, she tiptoed to Anna's office. Anna stared out of her window, her usually straight hair wavy and unkempt. Even her shirt was wrinkled.

It took two knocks to break Anna's spell, only for a moment after which she returned to her daze. Sue frowned, and her shoulders slumped.

A moment later, she dashed out of the office, wiping her tears. She wanted to fix Anna, even if it meant reuniting her with Jason. Crazy? Yes. Vile? Not. As soon as she sat down, she phoned her friend, Juan. A date, even if blind, would help Anna get over Jason. Luckily, Juan agreed, and Sue's eyes lit up. After she hung up, she buried herself in her articles. Hours passed.

As a yawn formed on her lips and the sun set, Sue peeked down the hall at Anna's office beaming with light. Perhaps the two of them were alone.

Sue pattered her fingers on her desk before opening the messenger, finding Anna, and typing: *Coffee?* When an ellipsis appeared signaling Anna was typing, Sue bit her lips, her heart racing. Flashed on her screen: *Sure!* And Sue smiled and clasped her hands. Anna sent another instant message: *Only here in the kitchen. Not outside.*

A minute later, cups were filled, and Sue dug for answers in Anna's sullen face.

When she asked if Anna was okay, Anna burst out crying and melted into Sue's hug. Sue's eyes shimmered as she patted her back. "It'll be okay whatever it is."

"Really?" Anna tore herself from Sue.

"What's wrong?"

Anna paced the kitchen and told Sue about how lonely she was without Jason, about Desiree, every little detail. Sue reassured Anna she would help her. After seeing her off at the elevator, Sue packed her own belongings and jumped when her phone rang with a new number.

Hastily, she answered.

"You were right, Sue. He's having an affair, and I don't even know her name," a voice squeaked.

Sue stared at the number again with wide eyes. "Isabella?"

"How many women do you know whose husbands are involved with your friend?"

Sue chuckled, glancing around.

Only after ensuring she was alone, did she plop into her chair and grip its armrest.

She switched the phone to the other ear and whispered, "I guarantee they aren't in touch." Anna's tear-stained face came to mind.

"I know. But he's in love with her. He told me everything in the middle of our date. He's changed and moved on. I can see it in his eyes. He'll find her, and my marriage—"

Sue sat up. "No, Isabella. I won't let that happen."

"How can you be sure?"

"I assure you. Now go on; it's late. Get back to your date night with Jason and keep him occupied. I'll take care of Anna."

"You promise?"

"The purest, most innocent one: a pinky promise."

Sue ended the call and flipped her laptop lid back on, its light casting shadows on her glasses. She googled Desiree and found she used to live in Hawaii. An idea sparked, and she dialed Anna's number.

The Invitee and the Host

Jason's Home
A Few Months Later

JASON'S PHONE BEEPED, and he silenced it once again. While securing one hand on his squirming son's stomach and reaching for a fresh diaper with the other, he sighed and fitted it around Josh's waist. "There." He smiled. "Little guy, my entire life depends on Monday."

He lifted Josh and marched down the stairs into the family room. Sue and Isabella talked to each other in the kitchen. Sue was outgoing, indeed. A faint smile formed on his lips as a shadow of his neighbor glided toward him.

A tap startled him. "Jason, you came?" Smirk danced on his neighbor's face.

Jason glared into his mocking, brown eyes with a straight face. "Why wouldn't I? It's Andrew's tenth birthday. *Gees!*"

Jason's son tore from his grasp and waddled away.

His neighbor chuckled and raised his hands. "Why that tone, Jason? We've known each other for years." He shook his head and passed around him to the counter, refilling his drink while Jason stared at Sue and Isabella. For two people meeting for the first time, their deep and long huddle in the middle of a bustling party distracted him from his neighbor's jabs.

He had invited Sue after all, not Isabella.

Sue chuckled loudly and waltzed to the drinks station by Jason. "Hi!"

Jason nodded and shifted on his feet, fighting the stiffness crawling up his spine.

She poured herself a cup of steamy hot cocoa while his neighbor joined a small group in the adjoining living room.

He coughed into his fist. "You two seem to have hit it off." He pointed at Isabella, who spoke to another guest as Andrew and his friends dashed past them, chasing one another.

"Yeah! She's lovely." Sue set her cup down and held his shoulder. "You are okay with it, right?"

A tremor of hesitation flashed across his face. "Yes. Why do you ask?"

"Just curious." Sue left with a smirk, heading back over to Isabella.

Meanwhile, Jason searched for Andrew. Oh, how he wanted to sit down with him and talk father to son. Yet the only conversation he'd completed at this party occurred while changing Josh's diaper. He bumped into other parents, dodging questions about his company and his family. The fracture of his home and work had become the talk of the town.

And he couldn't tear Andrew from his friends either.

The guests started to leave as Jason followed his little ones around. After bidding goodbye to the last family, Isabella cleaned, and Jason led his boys to their bathroom, preparing for their beds, happy to gain a few precious moments with them alone. Tucking them into their bed, he reassured them a million times that he would never leave them, hoping they would believe him. After they were sound asleep, he lumbered downstairs straight to the mudroom with a heavy heart and grabbed his coat.

Isabella's footsteps reached his ears before her frame did.

"Are you leaving?"

"Yeah."

She playfully punched his shoulder. "Come on, stay a little longer."

He shrugged on his coat and pierced into her brown eyes. "Did you know Sue Miller before this party?"

Isabella's jaw dropped, bursting into a peal of laughter. "Yes, Jason. I'm having an affair with Sue."

"Cheap shot." Jason crossed his arms.

"Yeah? Why's that? She's gay. It could happen."

"It could, but you're not gay."

She winked. "You weren't a cheater before. And yet, here you are." Before he could turn toward the door, she looped her arms around his neck and brought her lips closer to his. "Stay!"

He detached her hands. "The party is over, and I'll see you in court unless you want to settle things outside." He jerked away and marched to the door when her coarse voice halted his steps.

"You're just like your father!" she hissed.

He froze and shut his eyes, forcing a trembling smile to channel his fears, his failures, and his agreement with Isabella's scorn. After a heavy pause, he whispered, "See you on Monday."

And he slipped out the door.

Sue glanced all around and clutched her chest. "Isabella?" The home was empty. So, she rushed to the mudroom where Isabella glowered at the dangling back door. The washer was spinning and buzzing.

Sue froze for a minute before placing her hand on Isabella's shoulder. "Where's everybody?"

Isabella shuddered and whipped around. "Hi!" She shut her eyes. "Everybody left."

Sue brought her hand to her head. "Oh no! I did it again and outstayed my welcome." She slipped into her shoes. "I went into the bathroom for a while, but when I came out, it was a ghost town. Cake and sugar don't agree with me—"

"Stay."

A beep rang from Sue's phone before she shoved it further into her pocket. "What? No, no. This is embarrassing enough. You're cleaning already." Sue pointed to the spinning washer.

When she bent to tie her shoelaces, her phone dinged again.

"Do you have two minutes?"

"Of course." Sue rose. "Is everything okay?"

Isabella marched inside the kitchen, leaving Sue with her mouth open.

Two minutes later, she returned with an old photograph. "Is this her?"

Sue grabbed the photo and narrowed her eyes. "Yes. She looks much younger, but it's her. How do you have this?"

Isabella sighed and scratched her forehead, fidgeting foot to foot. "It's a long story, Sue, and you don't have time to listen to my entire life. Your cell has beeped multiple times in the past minute."

Sue pulled out her phone. "It's my girlfriend. She always calls before bedtime."

"Olivia?"

"Yes." Sue rested her frame against the dryer rack.

"From Hawaii?"

"Yes, the same one. Are you okay?"

"Not yet. What's going on with Anna now?" Isabella's hand hung limply by her side.

Sue leaned forward, her eyes widening. "Why do you ask? Anna is history."

Isabella sat down on the shoe bench. "Please tell me what's happening with her now. No questions."

Sue rubbed her mouth. "Olivia tells me she has a boyfriend named Adam."

Isabella lifted her head, and a faint smile graced her face. "Oh, that would kill Jason."

Sue shook her head. "What?"

Isabella rose. "I have hungered for this man's love all my life. And he's always carried her photos." She pointed at the picture Sue held.

Sue stared at the photo and back at Isabella.

"I found this one along with love poems a month ago, the same time he moved out. He has loved her since high school." Her shoulders slumped.

"But he married you." Sue straightened.

Isabella shook her head, gripping it with her hands. "Oh, but the gulf between his heart and his life contains my marriage. You can have that photo of hers, Sue, but I need a favor from you. The final one." She released her head and grabbed Sue. "It's wrong what Jason's doing. He's hurt me in ways I can't describe. No man should do this to a devoted wife. No man!"

Sue's mouth hung open, and she licked her lips. Her voice trembled. "What's the favor?"

"Tell Jason about Adam."

"Why?" Sue raised her hands. "He hasn't enquired about her in months since showing up at the office. Why risk rekindling his memories about her?"

Isabella released Sue and flicked her index finger. "Because I want him to know what it feels like to chase a pipe dream," she hissed.

"Anna's?" A tear slipped out of Sue's eye.

"Yes. You know how it feels, don't you?"

Sue nodded and gazed at her shoes. "What if she leaves Adam for him?" she whispered.

"You and Olivia won't let that happen. And tell him on Monday at noon. I want him to miss the hearing." She paced the tiny mudroom. "How dare he leave me and threaten to take my children away too! I've sacrificed everything for them."

Sue leaned on the dryer and rubbed the back of her neck. "He's done you wrong, and you're right. He must pay for all the people he has hurt." She lifted her head. "I'll let Jason know on Monday about Adam, but then he'll know how to get to Anna."

Isabella halted. "Let him! Let him go there, watch her in love with another man. He'll know how I feel."

CHAPTER 9 – LOVING ADAM JONES

"Love knows no reason, no logic. It simply transcends into a home, takes a seat, and mocks the heart."
Mars D. Gill

The Adam Dilemma

The Pink Bedroom inside the Villa, Hawaii
Presently, January 2014

THE OCEAN WAVES GREW so silent, I'd forgotten they existed outside my window. With the letters safely locked in my bedroom drawer, I marched to the shower and yanked it open. I entered without waiting for it to warm and pressed my palm against the wall, the water trickling off my shoulders.

My original plan of simply moving on in Hawaii wouldn't work, especially now that Adam had left. The letters were my least deceitful companion, and having read them all, I felt empty. Adam-less, letter-less, and soon-to-be without a baby—I shrank to the base of the tub and cringed into myself. Shivers sparked down my spine, and my hands traveled to my belly. I turned the shower off, rose, and marched to my cupboard. Without wiping myself, I slipped into my undergarments and khakis. For a top, my hands reached for Adam's checkered, buttoned shirt, its smooth fabric sliding through my fingers. I put it on, letting my wet hair dampen it.

Moments later, I put the purse on my shoulder and slipped into my outside shoes. Heather sat in a chair at the beach, fifty steps away. She sipped coffee and waved as I walked to the car in the driveway.

What did she gain from hiding the truth, anyway? At the door, I caressed the cold steel handle, unable to enter my car. I waited for her to stop me and scold me for scheming to murder a baby. In the living room calendar, I had darkened the circle on today's date—but she didn't utter a word. Was anyone going to protect my baby from me? I shut my eyes and opened the car door, avoiding looking directly at Heather.

Soon, I pulled out and drove south to the blue building under a canopy of palm trees on Kapaa's solitary main road. Kauai had a rule to not construct buildings taller than the palm trees. Somehow, they kept growing taller, and so did the structures. Rules were plastic.

When I parked at my destination, I stared at my phone, hoping and praying he'd called me. Nope. I shut off the engine and sat in my car.

My feet refused to move as though waiting for a steady hand to reassure me that I was right in erasing the only link to my past life.

I trembled out of the car and wobbled into the building, where I signed my name at the front desk and slid the clipboard to the receptionist across the glass pane.

"Abortion?" the lady with the thick glasses asked.

"Yes," I whispered.

She slipped more paperwork my way, clutching the other end. "Is something wrong with the pregnancy?"

Her hand fought me, but I released the paperwork from her grasp. "No."

"Is something wrong with the baby?"

"No." I scribbled on the form.

"Ma'am, Hawaii has the strictest abortion laws in the nation."

Finally, the person who would save my child. I ended my pen in motion. "I have researched the legal terms," I said in a weak voice.

She folded her arms. "You may have. But unless someone's life is in danger, only two of the eight islands will avail abortion services to you at twenty-two weeks. You will not find such a clinic in the whole of Kauai."

"You've got to be kidding me."

A hand pulled me away.

It was him, wearing sunglasses, shorts, and a shirt. I burst like a water balloon.

Adam embraced me. "I'm so sorry. An emergency crept up on me, and I couldn't get back to you in time."

The lady waited across the window and tapped the window, clearing her throat. "Do you have any more questions, ma'am?"

"No, we are done here," he answered, handing the unfinished forms back. "We're not going through with this. Please cancel." He pulled me and my fighting hand out of the building.

"Adam, this is my decision."

Once outside, he stooped on one knee, holding my hand in his. "I possess no right to ask you to keep your baby." He placed his other hand on his chest. "I'm nobody, but I wish to be somebody special in your life." He cleared his throat. "Will you marry me?"

My eyes widened. "What? You're nuts!" I extended my index finger. "Adam, you disappeared. Where were you?"

"Right after you answer my question." He rose, still holding my hand. "Do I or do I not have a say in what happens to the baby? Is she yours or our baby?"

I licked my lips, shaking my head. The words I had rehearsed to blast Adam with disappeared as I expected explanations for his absence, not a marriage proposal. "We met two weeks ago," I whispered.

He tightened his hold on my hand. "People spend lifetimes together without knowing one another."

I pulled my hand, but it didn't release. "Right. I know nothing about you, and you about me."

"I know as much about you as you do—that makes everything." He winked.

We laughed as the tall palm trees rustled in the wind, orchestrating soothing music. A few people emerged from the building, their faces long and pale.

As they entered their car next to mine, I whispered. "Marriage's first tenet is truthfulness."

He brought my hand to his chest. "Every second I spent away from you was torturous. I couldn't contact you, yet my heart and soul remained." He watched the car reverse and tugged on my hand. "That's all I'm at liberty of saying, especially without your answering my question." He tilted his head. "The baby needs a father. Yes or no? Will you marry me?"

I shook my head, staring at my shoes. "Where were you?"

"Answer me."

"Do I have a choice?"

He drew me to him and kissed me passionately. I had experienced that kiss before, like déjà vu—steady breaths, beating hearts, and his lips' tender caress delivering a calming reassurance.

I broke free. "I haven't said yes."

"You haven't said no either and . . ." He tugged on the fabric of his top. "You're wearing my shirt."

I grinned sheepishly behind my hand before clearing my throat. "I don't know how to be a mother."

"I know how to be a father." He held me close.

"You have children?" I stared right into his eyes, my forehead touching his.

Out came his signature smile.

"Are you married?"

He laughed more. "Do you trust me?"

"No." Not on my face, not even in my eyes, but deep, deep inside, relief washed over me, and I sighed. My baby was safe.

Adam moved in, his life contained in a single suitcase, making my short life in Hawaii feel big. Determined to pick up where we'd left off, I kept the letters and the one-off phone call from a stranger a closely guarded secret. Seeds of mistrust and insecurity had been planted in my heart. I feared I would lose Adam to my past, even for Jason, who had left me to write heartbreaking letters. My baby needed a father, and I hungered for a second chance at love.

But Adam led my mind to another problem he swore to solve: Desiree.

The first night we sat on my pink, flower-studded bedsheet, he got down to business, searching for her with only my rough, childlike pencil drawing of her. His focus was unwavering.

I extended the artwork with a broad smile. "I must have been an artist in my previous life."

Only a faint smile parted from his lips while he typed on his laptop. "*Voilà!*"

I sat upright. "Did you find her?"

"Five women named Desiree on the Hawaiian Islands alone!" He arranged the photos side by side on the screen and faced it toward me.

I glared at the fourth picture, unflinching, as my mind bounced from one disjointed thought to another. The photo held an uncanny resemblance to Desiree.

Adam rested his hand on my shoulder. "Are you okay?"

I rubbed my chin. "I'll be fine. You know what I noticed?"

He shrugged. "You found Desiree in these photos?"

I grabbed my head, shaking it and pointing to the fourth picture. "Yes, but not that." Lifting my head, I clenched his hand. "You don't call me Liz—or by any name, for that matter."

His eyes widened as he flung his hands in the air. "I just showed you Desiree's photos." He enlarged the photo with the caption, Desiree Darlington. "What does this have to do with your name? Now, focus! We may have found the woman who came in your dreams."

Air sucked out of my throat. Adam placed my drawing next to the photo, talking to himself. He opened her Twitter feed as I clutched my chest looking everywhere but at his screen. Had I grown up in Kapaa? "What if she isn't the right person?" My voice trembled.

"Do you recognize her? Is she or is she not the person you see?" He pointed at his screen.

Without a doubt, it was. "Yes, she is," I whispered.

"And it matches your sketch. She owns an antique shop right here in Kapaa, and we can visit her if—" Adam lifted my chin. "Are you okay?"

Tears rolled down my cheeks as I stared into his blue eyes peering at me over the rims of his glasses. "I'm worried about what I'll find." My letters said I had no friends or family.

"Why?" He embraced me and patted my back. "I'm sure everything will fall in place. But if you aren't ready, that's okay too. We can follow up on this later."

"Thank you." I released from his embrace, placed my head on his shoulder and shut my eyes, wiping away the moisture.

He ran his fingers through my hair. "Is there anything else you want to tell me?"

I opened my eyes. Was this man a mind reader?

I wanted to sob on his shoulder and empty my heart filled with haunting thoughts. And I wanted him to rescue me from the abyss of my negativity, but I needed something more. My eyes shimmered. "No, let's get some sleep. It's late."

Desiree Darlington

The Antique Shop, Kapaa, HI
Early April 2014

RELENTLESS RAIN washed over Kapaa for weeks, and the town glittered like a newly washed Lamborghini. Adam transformed our boring villa into a blissful sanctuary—his steady breaths while sleeping next to me, him playing with my hair and massaging my swollen feet. Adam . . . Adam . . . Adam . . . My life began and ended with him.

The only place I wanted to visit was the Kōke‘e State Park, where I'd written the final two letters and lost my memory, but Adam had locked today to visit Desiree Darlington.

The passion with which he chased my past should have been evidence enough for me to hand him my letters, but I debated endlessly.

Why didn't he envy my child's father or worry about finding him in his hunt for my past? But that was Adam—confident and sure of himself.

Bathed in sunlight, we drove to the antique shop, inhaling the aroma of wet mud and the freshly cut grass. When we pulled up, an ordinary building greeted us.

"Go in," Adam instructed. "I'll park and join you in a minute."

I seized my seat belt tight, my lips quivering in a pout.

He chuckled. "You'll be fine. I'll be right there, okay?"

I sighed and slipped out of the car as Adam pulled away.

Inside the shop, a wide array of antiques, from wind chimes to traditional clothes, were on display, and a woman much older than Desiree rang up customers. My gaze fell on a big, flat-screen TV, out of place in the shop just like me.

A diaper commercial rolled, and the camera zoomed in on a newborn's tiny toes. My eyes shimmered, and my hands instinctively rested on my stomach, hungering to touch my baby. Exhausted of hating myself for despising an innocent being, the longing made me human again.

The front door creaked, and Adam marched in with his hands in his pocket. "Shall we?" He extended his elbow as I slid my hand into it, our gazes locked onto each other.

He clasped my hand tightly and led me to the cash register.

The older woman now typed on her computer. "Hello! How may I help you?" she said in a musical voice.

Adam stroked my arm. "You may. My name is Adam Jones. Do you have a few minutes?"

"Yes." She rose from her seat and folded her hands on the counter.

He cleared his throat, releasing my hand and gently dusting the counter. "We are looking for Desiree Darlington—"

A phone rang, and she raised her index finger. "Please excuse me." She stepped away to answer it.

"You want to sit down?" Adam pointed to the chair by the register.

I nodded and took the plush seat.

While he studied postcards on the checkout counter, I caressed my belly.

Even though I couldn't picture myself as a mother, maybe I could make it work with a lot of help. I shifted in my chair and sighed. My left side hurt, and though I never felt her kicks, my doctor said that was normal for some women. When the cashier hung up, it took all my strength to rise and waddle up to the register.

"Who are you?" she said with a furrowed brow. Her phone rang again, and she silenced it.

"This is . . ." Adam gestured toward me and hesitated. "This is my fiancée. She and Desiree used to be friends."

"What's your name, dear?"

"I don't know." I gripped the wooden counter and scratched its surface.

"Excuse me?" The lady tilted her head.

Customers lined up behind me as I cleared my dry throat. "I lost my memory a few months ago." Adam patted my back, and a piece of wooden paint chipped, falling into my hand as I hurriedly removed it from the counter. "I remember nothing about my past except an image I believe is of Desiree Darlington." My throat swelled, and not an expression escaped from the lady's face. "My friends call me Elizabeth though. Do you know me?"

Her complexion grew pale, and a woman behind me sighed loudly, staring at her watch.

"I don't, dear." She reached under the counter and pulled out a picture. "Are you looking for her?"

Adam took a step back and covered his mouth with his hands.

She was the same person. No doubt. I nodded.

"How much longer is it going to be, ma'am? I've been waiting for a long time." The woman threw her hands in the air.

"I'm sorry. Can you step back, please?" the cashier asked.

Adam and I treaded to the side as she rang them up. He fidgeted beside me, staring into his phone. A sharp shooting pain shot up my left side again, and I held it, biting my lip.

"Are you okay?" He placed his hand on my belly.

I nodded.

As soon as the lady handed the last woman her bags, she said, "How long ago did you say you lost your memory?"

"About six months."

"Desiree has been dead for two years, my dear."

I coughed and clutched my throat. "What? How?"

"She met with an accident not too far from here, cracking her head. She died on the spot."

Adam held me as my feet gave way. "Who are you?" I mumbled.

The Wanted Baby

The Hospital, Kapaa, HI
Present Day

NO MATTER HOW MANY TIMES they asked me to breathe, my lungs fought me. I'd been sent to the labor and delivery room a good month early. Heather joined Adam and me there.

They shut the room's blinds, blocking the setting sun. Two nurses and the doctor stood by my folded legs.

"Breathe," Heather said.

"I won't. Bite me!" I yelled.

She raised her hands and backed off. Heather, the letter hider.

Adam's smile vanished, and he hovered over my head like an agitated fly. My life sped into fast-forward.

I pushed.

My baby came out covered in blood without a scream, and the murmurs died out. I lifted my head, my gaze glued to her being carried to the incubator. Was it my past floating away in red? Heather melted into a sob. Adam sank in a chair, not congratulating me or holding our daughter. I slumped my head back down. "W-what's wrong?"

"We are running some tests."

They instructed me to deliver the placenta., but I knew my hollow past had deepened. It was all freaking dead.

A mural of an angel with wings was carved on the ceiling. I stared at it through my tears.

A hand squeezed mine and the doctor's voice wobbled. "I'm sorry. We couldn't save her."

"What happened?" Heather stuttered, holding her head, wiping tears.

The doctor responded in a whisper as my frame sank into the damp mattress, my eye tracing the shape of the angel.

My breaths froze too.

Heather had shopped for my baby single-handedly and turned our safe house into a giant nursery. That house would threaten if we entered it without a baby.

Adam's face contorted and scrunched as he cradled his head beneath his hands on the sofa's back.

Words disappeared in grief.

My life. Gone! Not on the day of the accident. Today.

The next morning, Adam pulled into the driveway to our villa, having spoken no words since the night before. The truck came to a screeching halt under the same rising sun, the same resort, and the same roads. But everything had changed when we stepped out of his truck, and our doors thundered shut. We were home a day early even though it would take weeks for me to heal. The wounds on my heart? Perhaps never.

At the door, Dudley, Heather's boyfriend, opened his arms to her. She sobbed hard on him before marching to the dining room table. She sniffled, opened a notebook, and started to write what appeared to be names.

"What are you doing?" I grabbed the backside of her chair.

"I have a funeral to plan," she whispered.

When she faced me, her expression changed. Instantly, she rose and took me in her arms. "I'm so sorry, my dear. She was the miracle to set you free, the light at the end of the tunnel. I am so, so sorry."

Wiping my tears, I chose not to fight Heather on whether we needed a service.

She hungered for my girl more than me. An old craving for a nonexistent family beat inside her heart. I limped into my bedroom, where Adam changed his clothes.

I shut the door. "You're so aloof."

Standing across the bed, he removed his shirt. "I just lost a child."

"So did I! Or do you think I'm happy?" I crossed my arms.

"You need to rest, Liz—"

"Liz? Your behavior is too transparent. But from where I stand, I could have avoided all of this."

"Excuse me?" He tossed his shirt on the bed and tugged at the roots of his hair.

I slumped on the bed. "I know you and Heather blame me. But if I had done what I had wanted to at twenty weeks, that would have spared us—"

"You've got to be kidding!" He flung his hands over his head.

"You made me want her!" I shouted.

He picked the shirt and flung it over his head, continuing as though I didn't exist.

"You blame me." I pointed at him.

"Yes, I do! I really, really wanted this little girl."

After he bolted out the room, I plunged flat on the bed.

Confronting Everyone

A THROWAWAY TIME AWAY, a hummingbird trapped in a dungeon flapped and cried, no longer able to sing melodies. Me. A nameless nobody's mother.

I wept in my room, at the beach, privately and publicly. Adam consoled me in the days following the one where he'd stormed out, but he couldn't rescue me. Today, I wept at the breakfast table. I only had Heather keeping me company.

She passed me a tissue box. "I thought you didn't want her."

"Where did you get that insight from?"

"From your own words, my dear."

I raised my head and pushed the box away. "Or from the life story you hid from me."

"Liz!" She crossed her legs and grabbed the edge of the table.

"She was ALL I had of my bitter past."

"L—"

I almost toppled over my seat. "Hush, Heather. I've read the letters. Is there anything you want to fess up to?"

The curtains whipped in the breeze from the open windows as she gaped at me.

With Adam away on business, I grabbed the opportunity to confront her. We glared at each other, her eyes unblinking and filling with tears. Her lips fluttered, and she clasped her hands together as a tear trickled down her face.

"You said you're the mother I never had. Right?" My voice wobbled. "But tell me, why would a mother keep secrets from her child?"

"I lost the letters at the time of your accident." She reached for my hand on the table, but I pulled it away. "I've made my share of mistakes but not the ones you think I have."

"I found them in the drawer in your living room." I crossed my arms.

"You should talk to Adam, and he will explain."

"What?!" I rose.

She, too, stood, her hands flying to her ears. "Listen, Liz. I swear on Kāne I didn't mean to hide anything from you."

"I know what I must do. I'm going to Chicago." I took my uneaten plate to the sink. The caged bird would fly away and sing.

"Why?" She followed me, holding her belly. "I feel sick!"

"Jason Barnes. Why else?"

"How do you know?" She grabbed my arm.

"I called Purple Ink."

Ghastly silence followed. "The only place that company exists is in Chicago, and the only Jason who founded it is Jason Barnes." I wiggled out of her grasp and marched to the front door, sliding my feet into my shoes.

"Please talk to Adam first."

"I need to face the hideousness of my past . . ." I caught my breath. "And face who I used to be before I run away from myself."

Heather reached for her phone on the dining room table. "You don't realize what you're doing."

I jabbed a finger at her. "If you call Adam, this will be the last time you'll see my face."

Heather dropped the phone on the table and raised her hands as though at gunpoint. "Liz, my child, I will tell you everything."

"This time around, I don't need anyone telling me about myself. No! And don't worry. I won't run away from Adam either. I fully intend to inform him before I leave."

The Unwritten

The Spouting Horn
May 2014

AT THE MORNING'S HIGH TIDE, the tourists were sparse, and I held the cool metal rails. My dress fluttered and slapped my body like my soul trapped in a world of lies. Legend had it, a lizard monster breathed out of the Spouting Horn, one that had been tricked and trapped inside. I smirked—I'd chosen this place for its symbolism. Giggles tore through the wind gusts, and I turned. A couple parked their bikes and waltzed toward me, hand in hand. Seeing me, they stopped and slipped behind a tree, kissing.

How ignorant could love be for some people?

Beyond them, Adam shut his green pickup truck's door. I released the metal rails, overlooking the blowhole, and gaped at him. He had shaved and wore a black suit with a slender black tie, his hair gelled—a new man with a familiar face. He carried a dozen roses, marching my way. I waited to tell him I was leaving him and flying away in two hours. I had plans, but they didn't involve him. The roses bothered me, and I averted my gaze from them.

"Hi," he said.

Before I could face him, he took me in his arms and kissed me passionately.

For a moment, I forgot I'd plotted a breakup at the Spouting Horn, not a rekindling. The blowhole erupted as we released each other, cooling under its sprays.

"I believe we haven't met before."

A nervous chuckle sputtered out of me, my heart throbbing inside my chest. "I don't understand."

With roses in one hand, he extended the other as though for a handshake at a professional event. "Hi, I'm Jason Barnes."

My hands coasted to my ears, and I screamed. Suddenly, an urge to flee grabbed me, but he clutched me tight.

His eyes widened, his fingers slicing my arm. "Stay." He drew me closer, his breaths boiling wrath on my face. "I lied, it's true, but only because I loved you dearly and for you to not know me through the contents of those letters. I'm Jason, your Jason." He released me and kneeled, face suspended but the flowers lifted to me.

I stared at them through waves of my tears, rubbing the arm he had squeezed. The blowhole died down with only lathered puddles in rocky crevices, evidence the monster had breathed.

He shook the flowers in his hands, still kneeling. "Those letters you read, I brought them to Hawaii, not Heather." He extended his arm with the flowers again. "These are for you. I'm sorry you had to find out like this."

I snatched the bouquet from his hands, shaking my head. He lowered the other knee as though in punishment, his head hung low and arms by his side. The couple who was hiding behind the tree emerged. They cackled, his hand not leaving her as they glided to their bikes, allowing us solitude with the breathing monster. I wiped my tears and crushed the roses, letting the thorns prick my hands while he gripped his head in his hands, still kneeling.

Oh, how I ached to hold him and be held. But his tears belonged on his expensive, black suit. The words from the letters came crawling out from the burrowed recesses of my brain, dumping warm salty tears. The pain traveled and twisted my heart into a tight knot. "I can't—" I threw the flowers toward the ocean, and it landed in one of the black crevices.

"Please, Anna." He reared his wet face above his hands.

"Anna?" I glared at him, my chest heaving violently.

He stood and brushed the sand off his knees and legs. "I could never address you as Liz or Elizabeth, despite constant counseling from Heather. You were my Anna I lost twice."

I shoved him away, my tears dripping my dress wet. The blowhole erupted so high, we gasped.

He shouted over the splashing water. "By the time I located you, you had lost your memory, and heartbreak filled the letters, the only solid clues to your past." He grabbed my shoulder. "But Anna, I have loved you for over a decade even though you met me at a conference nine months ago. Somehow, this time around you noticed me. You never did in high school, the years I sat behind you, following you from class to class, day in and day out We were in the same grade but different sections at Stevenson."

I chuckled, gripping the metal rail and staring at the infinite ocean. "And we meet years later at a writers' conference without recognizing each other? How much had we changed?"

"You didn't. But I did." He stared at his boots, joining my chuckle. "It wasn't surprising you didn't make the connection. Anna was the prom queen who dated high school studs, not invisible geeks like me buried under problems. I couldn't muster the courage to ask you out."

I jerked toward him, finger pointed. "You know how much I hungered to be wanted by someone from my past?" Y-you were the father to my baby girl, and yet, you lied to me. Why?"

He grabbed my hands and whispered, "I didn't want you to remember me through the letters. They were only half-truths, even your name was fake in them."

I wiggled my hands out of his. "Are you saying I lied, that my words are false—"

"N—"

"When it's you who has lied all along." I bounced from foot to foot. "All these months, you were a married man!"

He pressed his lips together as though to keep himself from cussing. "You didn't lie. And I separated from my wife when I got your letters—"

"When was that?"

He pinched his eyes. "Last December."

I spread my fingers one by one. "August. September. October. November. Four months too late."

He gaped at me. "My heart belongs to you, Anna. It always has. I'd lost you a second time to Elizabeth, the person you had become after—"

"I can't do it. I can't forgive you." I clutched my head.

A jogger dashed to the rails, oblivious of the world breaking between me and Adam—Jason—the nameless, lying man in front of me. She snapped a photo as the monster sighed again. Neither he nor I looked away from our wet faces. We even stopped wiping the moisture off, letting the sea water mix with the saltiness of our tears.

He brought his hands together and shifted to one side. "Heather told me you were planning to go to Chicago to find me, and here I am, standing right in front of you. I won't blame you if you mistrust me now, and I deserve only misery." He licked his lips and pulled out his wallet. "You can verify my identity. Here is my driver's license."

I stared at his blue eyes instead, remembering his Adam smile and the dimples.

The jogger leaned on the rails but stole glances at us as I shoved his hand away. "Where's your wife?"

He slid his hands through his light brown hair. "My ex-wife and children are in Chicago, and the custody battle is ongoing. She has the boys until the outcome." He sighed.

The clicks from the jogger's camera distracted me. "How did you expect me to react to this?"

"I expected you to hate me, and it's painted in your eyes now." Jason stared at the jogger, who was now eavesdropping, until she looked away. "I deserve it, but I wanted you to find comfort in the fact that you weren't abandoned but rather cherished for most of my lifetime."

When the jogger stepped away, I laughed sarcastically. "You made a fake name, a fake occupation—"

The blowhole erupted again, and I marched away.

He followed and grabbed my arm. "Yes, a fake name, but the part about construction work was true. I lost Purple Ink . . . Never mind the details why."

"Jason, let me go."

"Wait. Please. I need to talk to you."

I shoved him. "You're fake. Just like Anna—Anna who?"

"Everly. I support your decision to return to Chicago." He clasped his hands again. "You can't start a new life without meeting yourself first. I just want to be there with you on your journey."

"Yeah?" I snorted. "Who's to say you aren't lying?"

"I don't know how to prove my heart to you."

"What else can you tell me?" I scratched my head. "Do you know my parents?"

He fumbled in his coat's inner pocket and handed me a piece of paper with an address. "On my last visit to Chicago, I found everything myself. I can take you there."

"That'll be unnecessary." I folded the paper and strode to Heather's car with him behind me before pulling out my floral backpack and handing it to him. "These belong to you."

Moisture clung to his eyes as he took the bag. "I'll wait for you here."

I slid into the car and slammed the door shut.

Turmoil was exploding inside me. Lies couldn't be untangled without letting go.

Anna Everly. A fool too. A name didn't matter. I would fly out, face my parents, and ask, "How many people attended my funeral?" Nine months of a missing person were enough to be considered dead.

Adam . . . my Adam. Not mine. And not Adam. Jason stood by the Spouting Horn.

He, too, was a lie. I sped away, letting my life slip away.

CHAPTER 10 – BECOMING ADAM JONES

"Falsehood flies, and truth comes limping after it, so that when men come to be undeceived, it is too late; the jest is over, and the tale hath had its effect: like a man, who hath thought of a good repartee when the discourse is changed, or the company parted; or like a physician, who hath found out an infallible medicine, after the patient is dead."
Jonathan Swift

After Anna Left

JASON SAT ON THE EDGE of the geyser, dangling his legs over the side. His coat lay next to him, right where Anna had left him, with only a stone securing it from the wind. His tie fluttered, and the blowhole kept erupting as though sighing for him. Hurried footfalls alerted him to Heather's and Dina's arrival. Soon, Heather's hand warmed his shoulder, and he glanced up through his tears.

"She's gone." She sat between him and Dina.

Dina shouted over the splashing water. "Heather, we had warned you to tell her the truth!"

"Did you too?" Jason scratched his cheek. "Anyway, I have to do what I should have done a long time ago. Are you with me, Heather?"

Her pale face faded further. "With you on what?"

"Fixing this mess. You lost the letters at the hospital, only for them to show up at my doorstep." He scratched his chin. "Then you blame Olivia. Why?"

Dina sat upright and extended her index finger. "Olivia was spreading rumors about Liz and her past life never having met Anna before. I told Heather the night you visited, soaked from the rain."

The blowhole erupted.

"The day I came to the villa for the first time? *Gees*!"

One stormy day, after Last Wishes night, Heather returned with the women to the shelter of their safe house, each retiring to their bedroom. Except Dina and Heather.

"Olivia's saying Liz is a home breaker, and a married man knocked her up." Dina stroked her head. "But how would she know?"

Heather's breathing hastened as the missing letters, which she had read, flashed past her eyes.

The doorbell rang, and Heather jumped in her seat before trudging to the door. "Who can it be in this weather?"

Dina followed.

Outside, wet and carrying a bag on one shoulder, Jason shivered as rain washed over him. He waved. "I'm Jason Barnes. I'm looking for Anna Everly." He craned his neck to peek inside, then reached into his pocket for a wrinkled, taped photograph: the spitting image of Liz.

Hesitatingly, Heather stepped back, allowing him to enter while Dina stood behind her with her mouth hanging open. "You know her?" She pointed at the photograph, following him to the couch.

Jason sneezed and held the couch's backside, still carrying his bag and staring at the dripping picture in his hand. "I've known her for ages."

Dina's eyes widened, searching Heather's face that gave nothing away. Heather slammed the door shut, marched to the kitchen, and busied herself dipping a tea bag in a cup of warm water, narrowing her eyes at Jason.

He dropped his bag by the couch and slumped onto it, blowing the photo and shaking it dry.

Dina took the lone seat nearby as Heather placed the steamy tea on the table in front of him. "Drink."

He smirked, but without questioning her, he devoured the cup down in one smooth swig.

Heather folded her arms and tapped her foot. "How did you find us? We're not on any map."

"You sure are. Roads come here." He sneezed again and placed the empty cup on the table.

"What is 'here'?" She pointed to the ground. "This is the Kapaa Beachfront Resort."

"This is a safe house inside the resort." Jason surveyed the room with his eyes. "Where is Anna?"

"You tell me the person's name—"

He rose, his hands extended. "Calm down, Ms.?"

She tightened her crossed arms. "Hiwalani. People I dislike call me that."

Jason chuckled and turned, walking along a wall boasting certificates for the Lion-Hearted Women of Kapaa. "You have ads placed all over looking for Anna's relatives."

"She is Liz now, and you'd better address her by her new name." Heather's heart missed a beat. What if the letters didn't belong to Liz?

"Hiwalani, you are looking for a relative." He spread his hands a little, glancing from Heather to Dina. "Well, here I am."

"How are you related to Liz?"

He shook his head. "Listen, you can't kidnap a person and keep them from their loved ones."

Heather rolled her eyes. "Oh, I'm scared. File a police report, and you'll find how incompetent that department is."

Jason pointed at the wall he had just lined. "Listen, your certificates are commendable, taking care of women and sheltering Anna. But now I'm here and can take it from here."

He shifted on his feet. "Is she okay?"

"How are you related to her?" Batting her eyelids, she stared at her feet while Dina rose and placed her hand on her shoulder. Heather didn't need more proof than Liz's old photo in his hands and his name that matched the letters. But she wasn't willing to trust Jason. In her eyes, he was a man from whom she had to keep Liz safe.

Jason stood across from them with the couch between them. "I-I love her."

"And you knocked her up!"

His mouth fell open. "What?"

"And left her here to die with no memory!"

Thunder gurgled, and he crawled to the couch and fell on it. "*Eh . . . ah . . .*" He shivered.

Unable to suppress the mother's heart beating inside her, Heather rolled her eyes and whispered, "You want me to get you dry clothes?"

"No, thank you."

She uncrossed her arms. "I've got no problem with you contracting pneumonia. It's my wet couch I'm worried about."

As Jason rose, Dina shook her head, rushed inside, and returned with a bunch of towels.

Jason declined. "I need to see Anna now. Before you say no . . ." He rushed to his bag and pulled out a floral tote that made her eyes pop.

Heather gasped, blood rushing from her face. She sank into the nearest chair. "H-How did you get these?"

Dina shot to the armrest sliding her arm around Heather, who had clutched her chest.

Jason placed the floral letter bag on the table. "I got them in the mail. You said she lost her memory. I can help her—"

"No, Jason. I think you should leave her alone. Really!" She pointed at the bag. "And you can't put those letters on the table."

He chuckled. "They don't have a hidden bomb, Ms. Hiwalani. You want me to abandon Anna?"

Dina whispered something, but Heather shushed her.

When Heather gave him no excuse, Jason's shoulders sagged, and he placed his business card next to the letters before plunging back into the rain.

As soon as the door closed, Heather snatched the letters and stuffed them inside the dresser by the front door.

Dina shook her head. "I don't get it. We've been waiting for someone to show up for Liz for so long. Why would you turn him away?"

Heather grabbed Dina by the shoulders. "Now is not the time to talk about that. I need to sort this." She scurried to Olivia's room and yanked on the lights.

As Olivia bolted upright, Heather grabbed her ear.

Olivia ejected a river of tears. "What did I do?"

"You mailed Liz's letters, didn't you?"

Olivia freed her ear and rubbed it. "Hell no."

Dina covered her mouth, bouncing from foot to foot.

Heather jabbed her finger. "Don't you lie to me, you little lowlife! I sheltered you. How dare you steal from me?"

Olivia clenched her teeth. "If I had to steal, why would I steal letters?"

"Then why are you spreading rumors about Liz?"

Heather's chest heaved barraging Olivia with questions for hours.

But Olivia insisted she had nothing to do with the matter, tears streaking her cheeks.

Presently, Jason whispered, "I know how Olivia found out about Anna."

"How?" Heather shot upright.

He glowered plucking a stone from the ground and tossing it into the blowhole.

"I said, 'How?' "

He sighed. "When I went to attend Andrew's birthday party and the first hearing, Anna's colleague Sue Miller told me she saw Anna in Hawaii with another man."

"Wait!" Heather covered her mouth. "When Isabella alleged domestic abuse against you?"

"Yes." He ran his hands through his tousled hair. "Thanks for the reminder. Anyway, Sue told me about Adam. Except she couldn't have visited Hawaii as she claimed—"

Heather gasped. "Of course! She would have recognized you."

Jason smirked. "Exactly. Someone fed Sue the information on Adam."

The three of them rose. Dozens of people cluttered the blowhole now that the sun had risen. Dina scratched her head while they headed to Jason's pickup truck. "Sue Miller. The name sounds very familiar."

Heather halted, her eyes widening. "Oh, dear. Olivia's partner!"

At the truck, a sad smile plastered on Jason's face as he played with the door handle.

"I can't believe I missed such a big clue." Heather clutched Jason's arm. "Where's Sue now?"

Jason's shoulders slumped. "Perhaps collaborating with my wife," he whispered.

Dina grabbed his other arm, narrowing her eyes. "Are you okay?"

When he glanced up at Dina, tears clung to his eyes. "I've lost everything today: my marriage, my children, my company . . . and Anna." He fluttered his eyelids and glanced up at the sky.

"Anna will return." Dina patted his arm, her eyes shimmering before she cleared her throat. "Sue and your wife are friends?"

"Yes, I learned when Sue feigned an emergency right before my first hearing to tell me the news about Adam, making me miss it." He leaned against the truck. "Even so I don't get why Olivia would mail me the letters, especially since Isabella didn't want to divorce."

Heather took Jason in a big bear hug as he sobbed on her shoulder. "It's my fault. I forced you to lie, but I was wrong."

He tore himself and dried his face. "Nothing would have changed if you'd introduced me as Jason. She'd still be gone. Even if she had the letters from day one."

"How can you be so sure?"

"That is what Anna does. She needs time." Jason opened his door and stepped in. "Are you coming? I can give you two a ride home."

As Heather entered behind them, Dina circled the truck and buckled herself next to Jason. She scrunched her forehead. "Is Anna going to see Sue in Chicago?"

"Very likely."

Heather grabbed Jason's seat. "We must warn her."

Jason stared at Heather through the rearview mirror. "No one is saying anything to her." He raised his index finger. "No more half-truths with Anna. We need to investigate first. Heather?" He frowned at her, still through the mirror. "Do I have an agreement?"

Heather nodded before dropping her head in her hands.

As Jason pulled out of the parking lot, Dina stared at her hands, shaking her head. "I can relate to Anna. Sometimes, you must see things for yourself. But I still don't understand the sense in hiding behind a fake name. Was this façade of name change a loyalty test?" She glared back at Heather

Jason found a room in the Kapaa Beachfront Resort near the villa. He wiped moisture off his eyes all night, sighing deeply. An image, one from twenty-some years ago, filled his mind. *Jason, you must get me out. I don't belong here.* His mother's voice rang in his ears into the wee hours of the morning, and he shot up in his bed. The responsibility of life overwhelmed him. As soon as he'd read Anna's letters, he packed his bags and left without saying goodbye to his boys. Just like his father. But he'd return for his babies.

Anna's final letter described Kauai. Though, only sure of her visit to the Kōkeʻe mountains, he'd arrived and circled the local markets fruitlessly until he stumbled across a flyer with Anna's photo—the first clue something major had happened. She'd lived here as someone other than Anna, not remembering her love for him as though their affair had never happened. He climbed out of bed and crashed on the rocking chair. When his silent phone rang, he nearly fell.

"This is Hiwalani. Do you know any of Liz's family members or friends?"

"You mean Anna's. But no, I don't."

"Dear Kāne! Liz is adamant on aborting 'your' baby."

Jason rose from his reclined position. "You have to stop her. That's my baby."

"Exactly!"

Jason moved the receiver away from his ear.

Heather cleared her throat. "You must come to see her. Just not as Jason."

"I don't understand." He paced the room.

"You can't approach her as Jason Barnes, who devastated her."

"But I didn't hurt—"

"Do you want to see her or not?"

Jason froze. "I'm in, Ms. Hiwalani."

"You must start with a clean slate. We can call you Adam Jones."

"That's ridiculous." He chuckled.

"You'll be my cousin."

"Really?" He slumped back on the rocking chair. "How old do you think I am?"

"And find a different profession. Show me you are committed to Anna instead of your wife and your sons."

"Is this a loyalty test?" He tilted his head.

"Yes, and I'm not giving you a choice." She breathed heavily. "I want to find out one more thing."

"What?" He slid deeper into his chair, staring at the ceiling.

"Name is immaterial. Memory is fleeting. But love lingers. Does she remember her love for you?"

A lie, a fraud, he'd become. He prevailed as Jason only on paper, hungering for Liz to remember Anna and her love for him, even if she had forgotten his face. The wanted life remained at arm's length and yet out of reach. Shuttling between Chicago to oversee divorce proceedings and Hawaii to pursue love under the garb of a lie became his life's unwanted truth. In January, he flew to Chicago and met his boys for the first time since he'd left. Tears. Complaints. Questions. All of it followed. Jason attended Andrew's tenth birthday and found out his boys were being fed hate stories about him. On the morning he'd to return to Hawaii, the police showed up at his hotel with a warrant for domestic abuse.

Isabella had unleashed her wrath. He made bail but was forced to resign and sell his firm, his baby. The life he'd built in Chicago capsized.

And now, driving back to the safe house alone with Dina and Heather, his dry eyes hid his sorrow.

CHAPTER 11 – CHICAGO

"Thou know'st the first time that we smell the air we wawl and cry. When we are born, we cry, that we are come to this great state of fools."
William Shakespeare

Ghost #1 – The Mother

IT WAS THE FIRST TIME I laid eyes on my home from an airplane before landing. The city of Chicago under the clouds. Lake Michigan's blue shimmering water. The spinning Ferris wheel. Cars rolled on packed highways, and when clouds interrupted my view, I craned my neck around.

"First time?" my neighbor asked.

"Yes," I said without tearing my gaze from the window.

Soon the plane descended below the intermittent clouds and circled Lake Michigan, studded with their shadows. Nervous energy bubbled inside me, and heavy breaths left my mouth. I forgot how to blink. A bustling city enlarged beneath me. Was it home?

"It's a great city, *eh*?" the big man in the middle seat, my nosy neighbor, said.

I grew up and lived here, but today, I was a tourist in my own town.

When the airport lights glittered into view, I gripped my seat handles tightly and pinched my eyes before the plane landed.

An eerie silence buzzed in my ear as I trotted outside the plane to the underground rental shops. Awaiting my turn at the rental car facility, I tapped my foot.

Alone in a strange place, I reassured myself all would be okay, that I was adequate for myself. I needed no one. As I grabbed the keys to my car, I reminded myself I would meet my parents soon, and the loneliness would wash over with joy.

But when I pulled out of the airport into the packed highway, the sun had descended and so had my rigor of reuniting with family.

I swallowed and checked into a lonely motel instead.

A gentle breeze whistled through the open windows of my rental car as I sat in the parking lot of an old brick apartment building the next day. Children speaking Spanish ran to a bus stop. Potholes peppered the lot and the road leading there, west of the Des Plaines River. I couldn't sit any longer, so I hopped out of the car and trembled to the apartment on the first floor. Upon ringing the bell, I cleared my throat, smoothing my plain, dark blue dress. It didn't ease my anxieties.

The beat of footfalls brought a shadow under the door. When the door creaked open, a woman held a lit cigarette. Scant, ruffled dark hair that stuck out a good six inches, doubtfully intentional, covered her head, her skin smooth but yellow.

"Anna?"

I choked on my lumpy throat. "Yes, and who're you?"

She chortled. "What? I'm your mother!" Boisterous laughter erupted from her, revealing brown teeth.

If that were true, why did we stand outside? I rubbed my chest, worried I chased another lie. This woman wasn't old enough to be my mother. "May I come inside?"

She cleared her throat several times. "Yes, you can come in, but it's dirty. I wasn't expecting company, if you know what I mean."

I followed her. Stained walls of the apartment gave it a third-world touch. Utensils piled high in the kitchen, and garbage sat alongside the counters.

"Aren't you too young to be my mother?" I asked as soon as I sat on the tattered couch by a grand TV blasting a reality show.

"I get that a lot. I was young and naïve when I had you." She grabbed a remote and lowered the volume.

"Do you live with my father?"

The woman snorted, extinguishing her cigarette on the ashtray. "No, your father was the first of my loves. I stopped counting after ten." Hiccup-like laughter. She plucked clothes from the floor and dumped them into a pile in a corner.

I tucked a loose strand of my hair behind my ear. "Do you live alone?"

"No, Drew is out walking the dog, but he'll be back."

I nodded. "What's your name?"

This time she held her belly when she laughed, seating next to me on the couch. Did my disorientation amuse her? I scooted an inch away.

"Elizabeth. You forgot already?"

I gasped at her name before composing myself. "I lost my memory in an accident, and I'm here to find my past."

"Oh. I wondered why you'd bother checking on me, someone in need." She brushed the dust off her arm.

A pause lingered. I hadn't expected this woman to be my mother. Heather fit that role much better. My letters said I had no family or friends . . . and Jason had called them half-truths. I scratched my head, glancing all around, trapped in the real Elizabeth's filthy, foul-smelling apartment—with no semblance of a home or a castle.

I'd be a misfit no matter where I set foot though. I could have waltzed into a mansion, and my feelings of not belonging would remain.

I opened my mouth and shut it several times before sighing. "What do you need?"

She threw her hands in the air. "Meds, for one. My health is on a roller coaster, and my old man got laid off. I can't work, and I need—"

"Yeah, yeah, I get it." Sweat laced my clasped hands.

"So, how did you lose your memory?" She tilted her head, leaning forward.

"I have a better question." I folded my arms. "How did you raise me?"

"I didn't. Mrs. Everly did."

"What?" I leaned forward.

"I had no means of taking care of you, so I put you up for adoption."

I raised my index finger. "That's the only part of this conversation that has made sense." I too had an unwanted daughter . . . one whom I lost. The pattern proved to be a generational crisis.

She giggled. "Well, you're back now, anyway. Blood is thicker than water." She placed her hand on my knee.

Removing her fighting hand away, I shook my head and wiped a tear. My throat hurt with the ever-growing lump it contained. "Nonsense!" I clenched my teeth.

"What?"

"Where can I find Mrs. Everly?"

She grabbed her chest, suppressing a chuckle. "You came looking for your roots fifteen years ago too, after . . ."

"After?" I twisted my mouth and fluttered my eyelids, suppressing tears.

The door creaked, and a dog barked so loud it made me jump out of my seat.

Ah, the old man, my biological mother's boyfriend.

She rose. "Drew, look who's here. This is my Anna, the successful writer."

He awkwardly shook my hand.

"Sit." She pointed at the couch, staring into my eyes.

I shook my head, stepping toward the door. "No, I must get going. All I need is Mrs. Everly's address."

She tilted her head with a slit in her mouth. "Oh dear. Mrs. Everly and her husband died in a car crash. You told me that the first time when you came searching for me." She stared at her feet and whispered, "I must have disappointed you, as I never saw you again."

The lump in my throat burst. Out came the fountain.

My crazy-haired mother squirmed, and I raised my hand and dashed out into the whiteness of the day, the deadness of the cloudy skies, and the loneliness of this planet.

Sliding into my rental car, my chest heaved. Thankfully no one followed me.

My past was dark and hollow. I choked and dialed a number.

He picked up, and I swallowed my howling cries. He repeated his hello, and I savored the best conversation I'd had in a while.

"Who's this?"

I ended the call.

"Wrong question," I whispered before pulling out of the parking lot, vowing never to return.

Ghost #2 – Sue Miller

I HAUNTED THE CHICAGO ALLEYS—listening to Jazz musicians, taking selfies from Willis Tower, splashing water at the Crown Fountain, making faces at the Bean, and riding a boat. The city had reversed the Chicago River's course twice. In comparison, the river had become my sibling.

And then came a morning.

Dressed in black pants and a collared shirt, I marched along with the fast-moving crowd in downtown Chicago. Within minutes, I had to step aside and catch my breath. Hawaii had instilled leisure strolls into my DNA. This was new. Chicago's residents, mostly young, zipped from place to place with headphones in their ears. Some held cigarettes, but all raced as if they were late for a train.

I, an unwilling participant, gingerly scanned the area and joined the crowd, sticking to one side.

When I reached the bottle-green building, I tore from the train of people and stalled.

Do it, Anna Everly.

I'd been calling myself by my full name, hoping it'd stick after months of being Liz. I lifted my chin and charged inside, collecting my new badge. Clutching it, I climbed in the elevator, unsure of what I would find on the other side.

I adjusted my hair in the steel wall's reflection. Fresh red lipstick sparkled on my lips. Questions I had scribbled on a hotel letter pad were now etched in my mind. The door opened on a floor decorated with balloons. Strangers who recognized me cheered me onto the floor. I shook hands like a celebrity.

A young man nudged my shoulder. "Is it true you've forgotten everything?"

Another handed me a latte. "Do you remember how to write?"

A middle-aged woman with her hair tied back shook her head. "Writing is like riding a bike, impossible to unlearn. You just have to get on it again."

I smiled at them as Ian Brady, my manager and the *ChicagoGoers* magazine's owner, tapped my shoulder. "We had Jacob move out of your office so you could return to the same place. Want to see?"

I nodded in relief. Anything to get out of here.

I gasped upon entering an office filled with bookshelves and glass windows overlooking the clock tower. What an oasis to write!

Ian cleared his throat at the entrance. "Do you want a moment alone?"

"Yes, please."

He smiled and left the door open as I sat down on my big leather seat and rotated it toward the windows.

The swish of the busy cars barely broke through the pristine landscape. Colorful cubicles with plants were visible inside a neighboring building. An unnamed vacuum of emptiness toyed with my heart. I tore away, breathing laboriously while grabbing a stress ball from my table and squeezing it. Oh, I was so alone.

A head bobbed outside my office, and I waited. A thin, tall woman with a pixie cut and giant glasses stopped pacing. "Hi," she said in the entryway.

I nodded with a smile.

"So, you remember nothing?"

"Well . . ."

"I'm Sue Miller." She entered, extending her hand, her eyes popping behind her glasses as I rose and shook her hand.

Sue. Crazy Sue from the letters. We'd met at last.

"I report up to you."

"Hmm."

"You came from Hawaii, right?"

"Yes." I pointed to a chair, and she sat. So did I. "How do you know?"

"People talk." She fidgeted in her chair, and it creaked.

"And what do they say?" I grabbed a pen from a holder and clicked it repeatedly.

"Your memory is a hot topic."

"Did you know me well?" I put the pen back and crossed my arms.

She blushed. "Some would say."

"Yeah? What was I like?"

She released a breath, and her posture slackened as she leaned forward. "Always professional, an immaculate sense of fashion, excellent with words, and a perfectionist in catching editing errors."

I smiled. "You understood me well."

"I did. You were . . ."

"What?" I leaned forward and slid a notepad toward me.

Sue folded her hands. "You were going through a tough time when you took leave and flew to Hawaii."

A moment of silence followed as I recalled my letters. Sue had insisted I take a sabbatical, and I had so many questions for the "Sue from the letters." But I had trouble asking the Sue sitting across from me. Something was amiss.

She squirmed in her chair and folded her hands. "Did you meet your friend Desiree in Hawaii?"

I popped up in my seat. She just asked me about a dear friend who was no more. "How do you know about her?"

"You told me you had lost contact, and I helped you track her. You flew to Hawaii to patch things up with her."

That couldn't be right. I scratched my head. Hadn't I found out Desiree was dead? How close were Sue and I?

And why did I struggle to believe our closeness? Just like I had trouble believing my birth mother gave birth to me.

"You should go back and hunt her down if you didn't finish that task."

"Maybe."

"I could go with you."

My mind's voice chuckled. The situation was sad, and I was unprepared to trust any strangers filling the world. I doodled on the notepad.

She cleared her throat. "We went to the East Coast Writers Conference in Orlando before you left."

I started writing the details on the notepad.

She leaned over and peeked at what I had written. "Did you make new friends in Hawaii?"

I glanced up. "I did."

"Boyfriend?"

To my relief, Ian entered, culminating our rendezvous.

Sue shuffled clumsily shaking my hand before she left, and Ian escorted me out. And just like that, my time at the magazine drew to an end for the day.

After bidding goodbyes and making promises to return, I emerged from the building, the evening breeze frisking my hair.

A short train ride later, I suspended my legs off the concrete at the North Beach as pigeons swirled the sky, and the seagulls squawked. I stared at children making sandcastles and at the dog walkers gliding by.

Hours later, when the sun painted the soft, ice-cream-swirl-shaped clouds orange and red, I lay on my belly in my hotel bed and dialed his number.

"Anna?"

I hung up.

I needed to hear his voice without the threat of a conversation. I quickly rose and got ready for my next plan but only after confirming with Dina that Jason was still in Hawaii.

Ghost #3 – Isabella Barnes

I STOOD under Jason and Isabella's towering mansion. Disparate images flashed past my eyes—memories with Adam. Our first date on the bike, the expensive dinner, the suitcase containing his life. Acutely aware of the setting sun and their home's solid structure, jealousy burned in my gut, and involuntarily, I burped. Fixing my hair and brushing the wrinkles off my dress, I staggered to the front door. Seconds after I rang the bell, a curly-haired, gorgeous woman opened the door before she slammed it shut on my face.

"So, you recognize me." I placed my hand on my chest. "That makes one of us." I brought my hand to my scrunched brow.

Why would Jason leave a woman who resembled a cosmopolitan model for me?

It took mammoth courage to face my mother. This was a breeze in comparison—even with the slamming door. The evening wind whistled, and birds chirped loudly as I scratched my neck. "It's all right if you don't want to see me. I'll leave."

As soon as I turned, Isabella opened the door and reappeared with red eyes. "You broke my home."

I held my throat. "I'm sorry. I broke a lot of things."

She played with the wooden door. "Where is he?"

"Who?"

"My husband."

"I don't know. I left him."

She raised her eyebrow. "Do you remember?"

"Barely." I stared at my sandals.

"Why are you here?"

I kneaded my hand. "I'm not sure."

She stared for what felt like a lifetime. "Want to come inside?"

A smile parted my lips. "I would love to."

I followed her into her home, eyeing the immaculately furnished formal living room as she walked past it to their family dining room.

The polished home resembled a five-star hotel: high, vaulted ceilings, elaborate chandeliers, mahogany wood— I quickly focused my curiosity on my hands, not subjecting myself to face the world that would never belong to me.

I just sat on the corner seat of the table, my hands clasped while Isabella marched to the kitchen and brought me tea, taking a seat across from me.

"Thank you." I cleared my throat, stroking the warm cup. "I came here to see the part of Jason that isn't mine."

Isabella smirked. "Jason doesn't live here anymore."

I rose with my teacup and walked to the photo collage filling the dining room wall from ceiling to floor. Professional, life-size family portraits showed twinkling eyes, hugs, and cuddles.

Beautiful family, indeed!

Isabella continued. "Either I see my husband in these portraits or the courtroom. It makes no difference."

Across from the happy wall, through the giant windows, Lake Michigan's waves pounded the shore much like Hawaii, but the fluttering palm trees were absent.

Isabella followed my gaze outside, color fading from her face. "He gave you his love, unconditionally and irrationally. He never did that for me." With shimmering eyes, she faced me as I sank against the wall.

"My boys depend on him, and he used to be a doting father even though unavailable at times, too engrossed in his work. The news of his infidelity broke me, but I would never leave him. Then, I found poetry and your old photos. It was then he left us. Apparently, you wrote to him, too." She stared into her cup.

I sighed and returned to my seat, unable to soak in any more of the happiness in the frames—the joy I was unwilling to disrupt. My entangled life was simpler without seeing those mirrors. Could I bear to look at my reflection through their cracks?

She shoved her cup into the table. "He abandoned us and is fighting me in the courts. I gave up my career to be a full-time mom while Jason burned the midnight oil." She pointed at me. "He can't lay claim over the boys and dump me. I've invested my entire life to motherhood! Today is Friday. The boys are at my parents. It used to be our date night. Now it's my mental health day. So unfair!"

"I understand." With that, I set my still-full cup on the table, rose, and marched outside as Isabella followed me.

"Are you going to return my husband?" Isabella held the door as I reached my car.

My sad reflection peered at me through my window, and I rubbed it off without success.

I gave up and glanced at Isabella. "He was never mine to take."

I entered my rental and sped away into the night's darkness, wiping tears during the hour-long drive to my motel. Cold loneliness enveloped me when I pulled into its parking lot. The lump in my throat had become my solitary companion.

I reached for my phone and called him. After two hellos, he said, "I love you." I hung up, sobbing against the steering wheel.

The next morning at my motel, I jumped when my phone rang.

It was Dina imploring me to call Heather who had broken down. I fussed but couldn't risk her showing up at my doorstep, so I complied.

The phone rang, and after a click and a hello, Heather sobbed and hiccupped. "This is why I didn't want to tell you about the letters. I knew you'd leave me."

"Heather, I'm not leaving you, but I need to figure out my future."

"You promised me you belonged in Hawaii despite your unknown past."

"Don't you get it? I can't keep promises to myself, let alone others."

"Yes, you can. Live your dream life in Hawaii."

I clutched the wall as though it alone protected me from falling and whispered, "I went to visit my birth mother."

Deep breaths rang across the line.

"We have nothing in common except a name."

Heather burst out crying. Again.

I paced the tiny room. "She is a junkie, and I don't even have a name for my father."

"I'm so sorry, dear." She sniffled. "Please come back."

I slumped on the bed and held my head. "I can't yet."

"Why not?"

"Last night I drove to see his wife." I lay down.

"Jason's?" she whispered.

"Yeah." I turned on my belly and lifted my feet. "She's beautiful, confident, and absolutely perfect." I lifted my body and crossed my legs. "I saw their family portraits, Heather. And here I was, beading my life with Ad—Jason. So wrong!"

"Why wrong? He loves you. Of that, I am convinced."

"Are you listening? They are four people who need him more than I do."

"That still changes nothing. We need you here. He needs you here. Come home."

"I can't. I met my old supervisor. They want me back, impressed by the work I've done for your organization. Standing on my own two feet is important to me. And one last thing . . ."

Her voice became heavy. "What?"

I hopped out of bed and traveled to the window. "You must focus on yourself now. I have noticed Dudley getting impatient. He may not wait forever. Focus on him, please."

"Like you are focusing on Jason?"

I sighed. Heather proved inconsolable even when I hung up. But I wasn't leaving Chicago after just arriving. I packed my days with work to resurrect my past life. I had yet to straighten out paperwork at the local city hall and find an apartment. Money was no longer a concern. The pieces of my life were rearranging themselves, fitting into one another despite Heather's effort to keep them apart.

Wet, Jason paused along the beach, surfboard in hand while Heather dashed toward him.

"There you are." She grabbed her knees and huffed.

"As I am every evening. Did you hear from her?"

She rose and rubbed her chest. "Yes. Fly to Chicago."

"What?" Jason stiffened before marching away toward the parking lot.

Heather followed. "She needs you, but she's naïve. I don't want you to lose her."

He halted. A cord shook in his chest.

Nothing had changed between him and Anna. "I listened to you once before. I can't go to her, and if she's meant to be mine, she'll return." Jason marched faster toward his truck. "I've chased her forever. You don't understand what it is like to obsess over one person who keeps slipping away your entire life."

They reached his pickup truck as he thumped the board on its roof. "I need her to fight for me. Without that, she'll be as unhappy with me as I was with Isabella."

Heather grabbed his wet shoulder. "This is movie talk. Return to reality, Jason."

"What do you want me to do, beg her?" He removed her hand and marched to the bed of the truck before shoving in the surfboard. He grabbed a dry shirt and threw it over his wet body.

"Yes. You know she's still calling you."

"Calling and not talking, Heather." He passed her and entered his truck, slamming the door shut before rolling down the window. "I need her to profess her love for me. I need—"

"That's your ego talking." Heather grabbed the ledge. "When is the court date?"

"In three days."

"So, you can meet her then."

"I'll pray to meet her then." He turned on the ignition.

"God helps those who help themselves." Heather tightened her hold on the door.

"That line doesn't apply to love. We all love but not equally."

"I've warned you." Heather crossed her arms and stepped back while Jason smiled and zoomed away.

Ghost #4 – Chicago's Jason Barnes

I, ANNA EVERLY, was financially sound. Through online research, I found the other adopted Everly children, and thankfully, they recognized me. We had grown out of touch, and my story mortified them.

In my first month in Chicago, I rented a studio in River North, overlooking Lake Michigan. The view calmed me, and the police sirens matched my state of mind. I frequented the pubs in the Loop. Surely, I would meet someone new even if for a night with whom I didn't share the baggage of losing a child or breaking a home. I had assumed Heather would coax Jason into coming to me, but nothing happened.

A week passed where neither of us called the other.

My pub visits weren't helping either. The men never measured up to his dimpled, full-of-sunshine smile or his bright blue eyes. Or they reminded me too much of him.

I longed to write him a letter. How had he forgotten me so easily? Did he even care for me anymore? Awaiting the winter's lull in the middle of summer, I sufficed with the police sirens that offered me company during sleepless nights. On one such evening, I wore fleece pajamas and sat on the couch munching Oreos when my phone rang. I dove for it as I had done when Adam called before our first date. "Hello?"

A female voice spoke. "This is Mrs. Parker, and I need to talk to Ms. Anna Everly."

I didn't know any Mrs. Parker or anybody else. "Speaking."

"I'm Desiree's godmother from Hawaii. We met a few months back."

I rubbed my chin. "Oh, hi! Is everything all right?" I rose and paced my living room. The setting sun cast shadows on the wall, the row of cars on Wacker now blinking.

She hesitated. A few stutters were audible. "All is well, dear. I'm sorry I couldn't help you. You fainted after hearing the news of Desiree's death, and I never saw you again. Do you still wish to learn more about her? Heather gave me your number and said to reach out."

My throat parched. I remembered no words.

"You and Desiree were classmates at school. She spent time with the Everlys as a foster child but bounced from home to home. When she was in high school, I found her at the Greyhound station, baggage in hand and crying hysterically." Her voice broke.

She continued to feed me lengthy stories while I strode over to the window overlooking the boats' twinkling in the lake under the dark sky.

"Her boyfriend was a married man, and he stood her up that night. I consoled her and even asked her to go home, but she couldn't face you. I was childless, and I offered to have her stay with me—in Hawaii, of course—while she figured things out."

"Your story doesn't add up." I massaged my compressing throat.

"How so?"

"Why couldn't she call me"

"I don't have the answer to that question. It may be the drugs she used to consume."

A chuckle involuntarily tore through my mouth. "A good friend or anyone who loves you can't just stay away and not be there."

"I'm sorry, dear. Will you tell him I gave you all the information I had and to stop asking?"

"Who?"

A beep was audible on her side. "Sorry, I gotta take this."

"Wait, hello!" I pounded on my phone, but she'd gone.

I held my head and paced. Did she mean Jason? But why would he visit them? The cold air pressed against my throat, and my heart raced at the prospect of listening to his voice, fear gripping my soul. Surely, Mrs. Parker called to help me and not take care of him. I swiftly dialed Heather's number and learned that he was in Chicago. A lump returned in my throat. Maybe he'd come for me. Perhaps a manicure and a facial were in order. I wish!

I'd spent hours dangling my feet off concrete steps by Lake Michigan with a book, a block away from my condo. Children swished on rollerblades, and people walked their dogs. Then I saw him. He straightened his suit and whispered into his wife's ear, and she giggled while his children pointed to a ship far out in the lake, chuckling and beaming with joy. Me?

My cheeks burned, ducking down and covering my tears with my book before I quietly slipped away. Their image wasn't what I'd expected. Their happiness taunted me, even from far.

Despite my hunger to write him letters, I refrained. I threw away my old cellphone from Hawaii and got a new one, never calling him from it.

I made Heather take a solemn oath on Kāne, the most sacred of all gods in Hawaii, to never give him my whereabouts. The next morning, I rejoined *ChicagoGoers* magazine exactly at the same place I had left—alone, heartbroken, and teetering on the edge of disaster. Life was a great leveler. Even memory loss couldn't alter the trajectory of my life.

Soon, three months passed in Chicago, with a chardonnay here and a merlot there with total strangers in bars, flirting but never inviting them home. I celebrated the survival of those months by going to work bright and early, working on a pile of manuscripts. At ten o'clock, I wrapped up a phone call, standing and staring at the clock tower from my office. I had enrolled my birth mother in a drug rehab facility and transferred ten thousand dollars into her account, and in return, we promised to part ways, as I didn't need reminding that I came from her. Soon, I'd return to Heather and devote my life to social service. Anna Everly was successful but lived a self-involved life, severely lacking in relationships.

When I emerged from my office, thirty-seven candles lit a cake, and my team broke into a birthday song. Crocodile tears carved my cheeks, realizing it had been a year since I lost my memory and that I didn't even remember my birthday. I acted cool the entire evening, and when I walked out of the office, yellow and red leaves had set the city on fire like an artists' imagination. In the weeks to follow as the delight from the imagery reached my heart, the leaves fell and dropped from the sky the season's first snowfall, covering the tree's newly naked branches.

Blizzards howled, and our diverging worlds became a concrete reality. Jason Barnes became history.

Sue Miller's Secret

AFTER DECLINING twenty times, I agreed to join Sue for lunch one snowy Wednesday afternoon before Thanksgiving. The restaurant bustled with lunch-hour energy, and the buzz from the crowd competed with the music.

"Thank you for doing this," she said.

"Sure. We were good pals before the accident."

"We still are." Sue smiled and cut into her filet mignon, and I bit into my salmon with lemon capers.

"How does it feel to be in Chicago?" Sue asked with a mouthful.

I picked at the salad. "I'm learning to appreciate the city like other newcomers."

She chuckled. "That's strange. You belong here."

"Hmm."

"Have you heard from Jason Barnes?"

I put my fork down and gulped my half-chewed salmon. "Jason Barnes?" I played with the locket of my gold chain—the necklace that survived the whole ordeal and never left my neck—my solitary companion through thick and thin.

"Jason Barnes, the founder of Purple Ink from the East Coast Writers Conference . . ."

"You talk like I remember."

Jason was my best-kept secret, the ruler of my heart, who remained invisible to the world.

Why did Sue revel in the most intimate parts of my life?

She chuckled. "You're right. We met him at Orlan—"

"The Writers Conference." I folded my arms across my chest.

"That's right."

I titled my head. "Why is Jason important?"

"Well, you two . . . never mind." She looked at her plate as though embarrassed.

"No, please tell me." I leaned forward.

"You two were intimate at the conference."

"I haven't talked to him." I shook my head and picked up my fork.

"It's probably for the best."

I put my fork down again and crushed my napkin. Her words distracted me. Those who had lost their memory listened to conversations like a newborn, every word scooping curiosity from their core. "Why?"

"Never mind. I'm sorry for being snoopy. It's an old habit." She nodded. "But it's good that Jason is history."

"Why so?"

"Because he's married." Sue folded her hands.

"That should be a deterrent?"

She glared at me as I pushed my plate away and signaled to the waiter for a box.

"Of course, it should."

I smiled. "Memory loss is a deterrent, a real good one."

Sue chuckled. "True."

While she resumed eating, smiling awkwardly between bites, I packed up my food in a box.

A sprint of two blocks over the Chicago River brought us to our green building. When we entered our floor, resting her chin on her palm and tapping her feet was a thin, tall girl, none other than Olivia from Hawaii.

She split into an ear-to-ear smile, and it took me a moment to realize the smile wasn't for me. My head zipped toward Sue standing agape as though she'd seen a ghost.

Olivia rushed to her, embracing Sue in a giant hug.

I planted my feet on the ground and waved with a smile. "Hello, Olivia!"

Her smile disappeared, and she released Sue, biting her lip. Sue's face reddened beneath her thick glasses, pointing her gaze on her feet. "Do you two know each other?"

My mouth hung open. Of course she'd steal my line. "Olivia is my housemate from Hawaii, but I'd be happy to have you introduce me," I said with my widest, sincerest smile, hoping it would mask my anger.

Sue spoke in a weak voice. "She's my friend."

I nodded. "I'll leave you to it then. See you soon, Sue."

After striding inside the glass doors, I turned and hovered nearby. With a long face, Olivia gently pushed Sue away. Olivia was involved in a steady relationship for years. Common knowledge. I shook my head and continued into my office. My instincts now urged me to keep Sue Miller close.

She knew something I didn't.

The Monday after Thanksgiving, I waltzed into the office with a new purpose: spying on Sue. I typed on my keyboard, focusing on Sue in her cubicle outside my door.

Sometimes I trotted to the kitchen, pretending to refill my coffee to overhear tidbits of her whispering into the phone. By midday, I opened her HR file. She reported to me, so I had access. I jotted down her address. Sue left early today.

Curious, I packed my belongings and hopped on the CTA's red line, holding a piece of paper with her address. At her station, I disembarked, marched to her street, and found her narrow brick building. Lights were on. So, she was at home. I sought shelter behind a tree across the street and peered into the front room through the open blinds. She walked into the room with a plate and handed it to Olivia.

She said something, and both laughed while I leaned against the tree. When a person strutted by, I suddenly became aware of my conduct and released the tree, adjusting my purse over my shoulder.

Before I left, I faced the home one last time. A third person emerged. A woman. Familiar hair, but from where? She grabbed a wine bottle from the table and drank it from the nozzle. When she placed the bottle down, she looked outside, and my eyes widened. Isabella!

Isabella, his wife—the mother of his children—so polished and Sue, her opposite, in bright-colored jackets overflowing with pinned brooches, were friends. I had tossed and turned all night.

And Monday brought with it a pile of neatly stacked manuscripts my admin had printed. Work absorbed me most of the morning. I had to pitch my recommendations for publishing in three board meetings that ran until late afternoon.

At three o'clock, returning from my final meeting, a colleague sat in my office, and I sighed. She needed my consultation on her piece for the *ChicagoGoers* magazine.

That consumed two more hours and stifled my ability to spy on Sue, who went in and out of the office.

At half past five, when I reared my head and rinsed my coffee cup in the break room, the office was a ghost town. On my way back, I bumped into Sue.

She headed out with her bag on her shoulder. "Hey," she said awkwardly.

"I've been meaning to talk to you."

"You have? I'm late for an errand. Can we talk tomorrow?" Sue's color was pale even before I confronted her.

"It's not about work. I'm calling the police about the matter, but perhaps they can talk to you directly." I waltzed into my office.

She followed me, her backpack slipping to her elbows. "What? Why? What did I do?"

"I opened a court case in Hawaii related to my alleged accident. The trouble is, I don't believe it was an accident."

Sue's eyes widened, and her breaths became heavy. "What do you suspect?"

"I know who found me on the roadside." I gathered my belongings from my table.

"Oh?"

"Yes. And I think you do too."

Sue straightened and stammered as I flung my purse on my shoulder.

"Olivia and 'her partner' found me."

She fidgeted and ran her fingers through her hair. "Whoever found you along the roadside rescued you. Where is the sense in this witch hunt?"

"Sue, I know it was you." I held my desk.

The backpack fell from her shoulders with a thump. She glanced around, her entire frame trembling.

I clenched my teeth. "You could have revealed my identity and helped me when I was down and out. But you chose not to. Hell, you didn't even tell me—"

She rubbed her chest. "Olivia has had a lot of partners over the years. It wasn't me."

"I'll let the police decide that." I glanced at my watch.

Sue shifted from foot to foot, refusing to leave or say anything else. Exiting, I brushed past her at the door. As soon as I took three steps into the hall, a sharp blow to my head knocked me into a slow oblivion. Oh, freaking troublemaker, Sue!

Sue clutched her head and fell to her knees, the fire hydrant crashing on the floor. She buried her head in her hands and sobbed. "Sorry! I should never have followed you to Hawaii!"

CHAPTER 12 – SUE: THE TROUBLE KEEPER

"Now I am past all comforts here, but prayer."
William Shakespeare

The Day Before Anna's Fall

"I'M NOT DISTRACTED." Seated inside a quaint little restaurant in the heart of Kapaa, Sue compressed Olivia's hand.

Olivia's cheek flickered as she twisted her lips, staring at their twined hands. "I never dated online until I met you, but now that you're here, it's clear you're following that girl over there."

Sue whipped her head from side to side. "Who?"

Olivia freed her hand from her grasp and pointed to a woman with a book, sitting in a corner.

Sue coughed, choking as she hurled down her glass of water. While she'd come to Hawaii to bond with Olivia, her online love, she also wanted to check on Anna. Apparently, she'd failed to hide her ulterior motives. She shook her head with a smile. "Be serious, Liv. I'm here with you." She raised her brow. "Are you still with the nonprofit?"

Olivia straightened her back. "Yes. It grounds me. I know what you think about getting external help, but this works for me."

"But now you have me, and I'm great at helping others."

Olivia smiled. "What are we doing tomorrow?"

Sue glanced at her text messages from Anna, whose birthday was the next day. "How about the Kōke'e State Park?"

The Fall

Kauai's Kōkeʻe Mountains, Hawaii
October 2, 2013

THE HIKE PROVED REFRESHING and tiring at the same time. For an hour, they searched for a bathroom, but the road was devoid of businesses. Sue suggested Olivia go behind the bushes.

However, Olivia's face reddened, her hands jittering. "This part of the forest is cursed. I can't take a chance. What if the Menehune—"

Sue's eyes widened. "The mythical dwarfs? Olivia, you've got to be kidding me. You're a southern girl from Alabama, for crying out loud."

Hesitating, Olivia crept behind the bushes, and Sue kicked up dirt. A woman's singing grew, and Sue halted to focus, strutting toward the sound. Suddenly, Anna with arms spread like an airplane came into focus, and Sue sneezed into her hands. As the moist darkness of her palms deepened, tires screeched, and a loud thud followed. When Sue lifted her head, a dust cloud swirled blocking her vision before a red car appeared headed downhill. Another whirring sound alerted Sue.

She grabbed her chest when her eyes fell on Anna's bicycle that lay flat on the road, several feet away. Its twisted rear wheel spun as though in a circus show.

Further back on the trail, Olivia shouted out her name. Sue opened her mouth to answer, but her foot lodged on something on the ground, and she fell over it. She pressed her hands on the ground and lifted her body, releasing her foot from the heavy weight. When Sue turned, she screamed. A body lay face down behind her. Sue flipped it. Anna! Her throat collapsed as Olivia continued to call out for her. Trembling, she pulled out her phone.

No signal. She rose and paced, waiting for a car to flag down. Olivia's car was in the valley below. A little sliver of guilt tortured her soul. Had she caused Anna's accident? Sue had already been to jail once for drugs. She couldn't afford to go back.

She bent and shook her again. Miraculously, Anna opened her eyes, looked straight at Sue, and stuttered, "W-who are you?" before collapsing for the final time. Sue covered her mouth as a scene appeared in front of her eyes, where she scrubbed the bathroom floor in orange overalls under fellow inmates' nasty glares at the correctional facility.

While Sue grabbed her head and sobbed, Olivia charged toward her. "Sue!" Her flustered face deepened, and she dug her fingernails into her cheeks when her gaze traveled from Sue to Anna. "Oh no, no, no, no, no! No good can come out of this forest." She reached for her phone and punched numbers.

Sue wiped her tears. "There's no signal."

"It's ringing for me. Shush."

Sue rose, trembling. "Who are you calling?"

"The police, who else?"

Sue snatched the phone and ended the call. "I don't want any trouble, Liv. No police."

"What do you have to worry about?"

"I told you, no police. Are you with me or not?" She clenched her teeth.

"Then let me call Heather."

At the Kauai Veteran's Memorial Hospital, Heather held hospital forms as the emergency staff hurled Anna inside on a stretcher. Olivia and Sue huddled in one corner, whispering into each other's ears. When Heather took a seat in front of them, Sue nudged and Olivia asked, "Are you going to file a police report?"

Heather flipped a sheet of paper as though oblivious of the question as Sue's body stiffened. Scribbling on the form, she said, "Police report? No way. They never help."

Sue's body relaxed.

Heather craned her neck above the forms. "I'm waiting for the girl to wake up, and she can take care of it. I refuse to see any policeman's face."

Sue bobbed her head up. "Or a policewoman's face."

Heather swiveled at her with a frown.

Olivia elbowed Sue. "What if someone hurt the girl?"

Heather's eyes widened, putting her pen down. "You said you saw her fall and that it was an accident."

Olivia stared at Sue, and Sue scratched the back of her neck. "I mean, it happened so suddenly. The details of her fall have muddled in my head."

Heather flung her hands before picking her pen from the clipboard when Sue's gaze fell on a floral bag in Heather's lap.

She whispered into Olivia's ear. "What's that?"

Olivia shrugged and addressed Heather. "How are you filling the hospital forms, anyway?"

Heather grabbed her head, her pen dangling between her finger. "I don't know, but I need to find out more about the girl."

Sue's eyes swelled with never-ending tears. Every time she sniffled, Olivia rolled her eyes, but Sue couldn't shove a stone over her feelings. Repeatedly, she opened her mouth to tell Heather the truth, but a glance at Olivia's sullen face sealed her mouth. Their relationship's infancy stage wouldn't weather the truth, so she stared at her dirty sneakers instead.

Heather slung the floral bag around her shoulders. "You girls go now. Take my car and wait for my phone call. You can pick me up later."

"You're going to wait here?" Sue asked as Olivia turned to leave.

"Yes. I refuse to leave the injured girl here alone." She wrung her hands. "Hopefully, she'll wake soon, and we can contact her family."

Sue sighed following Olivia out with her head suspended.

Sue's heart and soul were imprisoned at the hospital. Within a few hours, the sun descended, and she returned to the hospital and froze, her hands traveling to her mouth.

Heather wept uncontrollably in the waiting room exactly where they'd left her. Anna's floral bag lay open and empty on the floor, and letters and ripped envelopes sprawled across her lap. Sue grabbed the newspaper from a table in front of her, opened it, pretending to read taking a few steps away. She came here to confide in Heather now that Olivia was in bed, but the truth got stuck in her throat. The double doors opened. A young, petite doctor with glasses made his way toward Heather, who frantically dried her cheeks and shoved the contents back inside the floral bag.

She rose and met the doctor, feet away from her chair and the letters. Instinctively, Sue rushed to the bag and collected it, hiding behind the newspaper.

The letters weren't part of the plan. None of it was, but she couldn't trust anyone. She rushed behind a pole from where she could hear their conversation out of their view.

The doctor shook Heather's hand. "How are you related to Elizabeth?"

Elizabeth? Sue frowned and pulled out a letter. Oh dear! Something only Anna could do. She grabbed her head and shook it.

"I'm not related to her," Heather answered. "My name is Hiwalani Keahi, and I go by Heather." She handed him her business card. "I run an organization called the Lion-Hearted Women of Kapaa. We help women in need. I'm here on behalf of it and will take care of Elizabeth until we can inform her relatives."

The doctor nodded, flipping sheets on the carboard in his hands. "I see you brought her in. Can you tell me what happened?"

Sue had to strain to hear the answer, Heather's voice barely above a whisper. "We collected her from the cursed section of the mountains."

Sue rolled her eyes.

"Excuse me?" the doctor asked.

"Where the king lost the island to—"

"Ma'am, we don't have time for legends."

"No one does nowadays." She sighed. "Anyway, we found her. The most probable cause is an accident on her bike, not that anyone saw."

He flipped a sheet. "Have you filed a police report?"

"No, is it needed?"

"Yes."

Heather crossed her arms. "Can't one of her relatives file it? I don't know the woman."

The doctor placed his hand on her shoulder, both walking toward the front desk with Sue's shadow behind.

The doctor said, "I doubt she'll be able to tell us much about her next of kin."

"Why is that?"

They stopped as Heather glanced back at Sue who hurriedly slumped on a chair with the newspaper being her only guard.

When Heather looked away, Sue sighed.

"Ms. Elizabeth has undergone a traumatic brain injury. She's out of a comatose state. But she remembers nothing, including her name. It can happen with brain injuries. She's unstable and breaks down easily. It's hard to predict if or when her memory will return."

With lips trembling, Sue slid a few chairs away toward the exit, while Heather rubbed her forehead. "Well, that's not too terrible, I suppose."

The doctor crossed his arms. "There's more. Ms. Elizabeth is about ten weeks pregnant."

Sue dropped the newspaper, tears streaming down her naked face.

Heather was too busy to notice as she grabbed the doctor's arm. "You said 'is.' Does that mean the baby is okay?"

"Yes, so far. But we must watch for a few days."

She steepled her hands. "I or one of my girls will be here every day until her memory returns, and we will crowdfund her expenses. Please take care of Elizabeth as best you can."

Sue rose and teetered out with the floral bag. When she reached the exit, away from Heather's sight, she dashed out into the dark, beyond her parked car. On a lonely, unlit corner, she stooped and caught her breath. Her parched throat ached, threatening to collapse. She frantically scrambled for her phone and dialed a phone number.

"Hi Isabella." She panted.

"Who is this?" spoke a muffled voice.

"It's Sue from Hawaii. I came here chasing Anna, remember?" Sue gripped her stomach with one hand.

"Sue? Anna who?"

"Jason's mistress." Sue lumbered back to her car and leaned against it.

A pause, then Isabella coughed. "Yes. I'm sorry. It's midnight here."

"Is he next to you?"

"No, he's in the other room. What's wrong?"

Sue circled the vehicle. "Well, I came here following Anna, keeping her away from Jason as I had promised—"

"Wait a minute." Her pitch rocketed. "I didn't ask you to take her to Hawaii. Are you in trouble?"

"Well, not exactly. Anna—"

"What?"

"She was in an accident, I think, and got hurt. She lost her memory, at least for now."

"I shouldn't have trusted you." Isabella took labored breaths. "I didn't ask you to fly to Hawaii, and I have nothing to do with this!"

Sue ground her teeth as heat flushed through her body. "Well, Anna is pregnant with his baby."

A ghastly silence followed.

Sue gritted her teeth, whispering, "Jason must pay for his actions. It's the right thing to do."

"Have you gone insane, Sue?" Isabella's voice grew so loud Sue had to rub her ear under the phone. "Who knows whose baby it is? And why is it you suddenly have a conscience?" She hissed. "If you tell Jason, it'll ruin my marriage."

"It's the right thing to do. I can't leave the poor girl here alone." When Heather come out of the hospital, Sue entered her car and hid the tote under her seat.

"What do you want? Money? Please, Sue. You can't do this." Isabella's voice had softened.

A nervous laugh escaped Sue as she straightened. "Do you think I'm a sellout?"

"Why else would you help me all along? What's in it for you to risk everything?"

"People have morals." Sue tapped her foot involuntarily.

Isabella breathed heavily into the phone. "Now, you listen to me. If you bring her back or tell Jason and hurt my family, I'll notify the police about you—your plan to travel to Hawaii, the accident. Everything. You'll suffer, Sue. I've recorded all our calls and checked your record. It isn't clean."

Sue shuddered.

A knock on her window made her drop the phone.

She hurriedly found it, turned it off, and stared into Heather's eyes, rolling the window down. "H-hi. I came to get you."

Heather's face was pale and deadpan. She lumbered around the car and climbed into the passenger seat.

Sue smiled, started the car, stashing her phone into the cupholder. Pulling out of the parking, she asked, "I-Is everything okay with the girl?"

Heather stared ahead listlessly and didn't utter one word through the whole way to the safe house, and Sue didn't probe more either.

When they reached the villa, Heather slipped out before Sue could say anything. She didn't turn around once, disappearing inside the villa.

Sue drove to her hotel, her heart heavy as a bag of stones.

After she parked and entered her room, she was relieved Olivia sat on the bed, working on her laptop. Sue rushed over to her and collapsed, sobbing like a child.

Olivia closed her laptop, stroking Sue's hair.

In the glow of the dim lamplight, Sue spilled everything to Olivia.

She told her Liz's true name was Anna Everly, and she was an editor who'd had an affair with Jason Barnes.

Olivia clasped Sue's hand. "It's not your fault. You were trying to help Isabella."

"Aren't you mad at me for fancying her?"

"You had a crush on her. So what? I have had my share of those."

Sue squeezed Olivia's hand. "That means everything to me. Maybe we should tell Heather Anna is from Chicago."

Olivia frowned. "Sue, she'll think you hurt her."

"Why?" Sue's lips quivered while she leaned back, scratching her neck.

"Because you found her and didn't tell us you knew her." Olivia looked at her watch. "Especially now after six hours. She thinks her name is Elizabeth, for Kāne's sake. They'll suspect your motives."

"You're right." Sue grabbed a pillow. "But how do I help her?"

Olivia's lips trembled. "Do you still love her? Because if you do, we are over."

"Olivia—"

"Me or her?" A tear fell down Olivia's cheek.

"You, Liv." Sue cupped Olivia's face before embracing her.

That night Sue chose to do nothing in order to prove her loyalty to Olivia. But worrying for Anna was her unshakeable companion.

CHAPTER 13 – THE BATTLE

"In every battle there comes a time when both sides consider themselves beaten, then he who continues the attack wins."
Ulysses S. Grant

The Stroke of Luck

Chicago
December 2014

THE BANG OF HIS HANDS on the cab. His interlocked lips. Sluggish gators. Him rotating his wedding band. The clouds dancing around wrinkly, green mountains. The red-laced shoes kicking dust on the road. I opened my eyes, pain crippling me as I wrung my neck, searching for Sue and cursing under my breath. But my head fell back into the floor's chilly embrace, and a faint buzz echoed in my ears only interrupted by hiccup-like sobs. Ancient images returned to me through a stroke of luck, or should I say a brutal attack? Through the periphery of my eyes, Sue's shape formed into focus. She held her head and bawled like a child.

Then a woman in a white, swishy gown marched in. "What did you do?" she cried, taking Sue into her arms.

Olivia.

"I was getting ready to leave for our big day. Look at you, Liv, so beautiful—"

"What happened?"

"She threatened to sue me for concealing her identity. I don't know what came over me. I just yanked the fire hydrant and smashed it over her head." Sue glanced at her extended hands and dropped them. "What should we do?"

Heavy breaths preceded a deep guttural groan. "Bury her!"

Sue grabbed her stomach, leaning forward as though to throw up. "What?!"

My heart raced, but I couldn't lift a finger.

"I'm tired of people like her who feel entitled. I lost my relationship with Heather, who was like my mother because of this girl. YOU"—Olivia jabbed a finger at Sue—"have spent the greater part of your last year in repentance, helping her in your roundabout way. You even had me mail the letters to Jason to reunite them! Today was supposed to be our day. We were to start a new life. And it's been ruined, thanks to her!" Tears streaming down her face, Olivia marched up to Sue. "I was waiting at the footsteps of the chapel. You didn't show up."

"I know," Sue whispered, hanging her head.

Olivia pressed on Sue's hands. "Our life will never begin if we worry about her. Drop her, Sue. Bury your past feelings about this problem once and for all. I have the cash! We'll move to Helena, Montana, and buy a piece of land. We can start anew. Don't let her keep us from our dreams."

Sue nodded, and my heart raced before I batted by eyelids.

Soon, a chemical-laced gauge, smelling of a sweet marker ink rubbed against my lips and oblivion firmed its hold on me.

Heather scrubbed the villa's kitchen counters for the millionth time in Hawaii. When Dina strode into the living room, her backpack slung on her shoulders, she frowned. "We all know you're not a clean freak. What's going on?"

Before Heather could respond, the front door creaked open, and Dudley, Heather's boyfriend, marched in. "Hello." He slammed his keys on the dresser.

Dina flung her arms. "Heather is cleaning again."

"I don't see how that is a bad thing" She moved to the stainless-steel fridge, wiping it with a rug.

Dudley marched to her and leaned in, planting a kiss on her forehead. "You know what I am thinking?"

She squeezed the rug in her hand, avoiding looking directly at him. "I can't say no to you a thousand times."

His smile disappeared, and his eyelids drooped before he sighed loudly. "What's your excuse now? It used to be your L—"

"Call her Anna, please. And she isn't mine."

She trotted to the dining table where Dina shoved papers into her backpack.

Dudley leaned against the fridge. "Right. You said you needed to help her and getting married was out of the question. Now that she's on her own, I'm wondering . . ." His glance fell on Dina.

Dina zipped her bag and flung it over her shoulders. "I was just leaving."

Heather held her shoulder. "Where are you going?"

"My forgetful *makuahine*, I leave in the morning, right?" She lifted her loose pants.

"I have shed a thousand tears I'm losing another of my daughters, this time to education. Need I the reminding?"

Dina chuckled. "No. But the university is in Honolulu—so close."

Heather flung her hands. "But where're you going tonight?"

Dina lowered ger gaze and whispered, "I'm spending the night with Matthew. Please, I'm terrible with goodbyes. That's why I'm doing this now rather than in the morning." She stretched her arms toward Heather.

Heather embraced her and whispered, "I thought you and Matthew went separate ways."

Dina released her and smiled. "It's our final goodbye. Listen to Dudley, will you?" She raised her brow and disappeared out the door with her bag.

Heather brushed the rug. "Dudley, my love."

He still leaned on the fridge, lost in a trance, shaking his head.

She set the rug on the table. "It's not you, Dudley. I promise it's me."

He trudged over to her and grabbed a chair's backside. "No words are needed, Heather, my ladybug. I understand."

Heather pulled a chair out for him. "No, my dear. You are getting it quite wrong—"

He shoved the chair back in. "Why would you not marry then? We're not getting any younger, and you're not as busy as you used to be. You consume all your time cleaning and re-cleaning the villa. Wouldn't you be happier to do something else?"

Heather broke into a hailstorm of tears. Her chest heaved with each gulp of air.

Dudley ran his hands through his hair. "I'm sorry, dear. I—"

"No, that's the thing, Dudley. I have more time because there's no business, and my debt is mounting." She wiped her tears but more fell. "The last woman I took in left the following morning because of a leak over her bed, and I'm running out of donations." Her lips quivered. "I'm organizing the same events Liz helped me with, but the turnout is pathetic."

Dudley grabbed her hand and planted a kiss. "Why did you not tell me before? I could have helped you."

"I'm a strong woman, Dudley. I run a safe house for women. I help. By no means, do I take help from—"

"A man?"

She pointed at him. "You said it, not me."

Dudley chuckled, drawing her into his embrace. "I can loan you the money to fix the place up, pay off your debt, and invest in your business."

"No. Its future is nonexistent." She freed herself, adjusted her hair, and cleaned her face of any residual tears while he leaned back and frowned. Staring behind him into a haze of nothingness, she continued in a resigned voice. "No more women remain in Kapaa who need my assistance."

"That's as untrue as the Earth being flat," a voice behind Dudley said.

Heather's eyes lit up. "Liz—Anna. You're back!"

I dropped my suitcase as Heather rushed to me, engulfing me in a torrent of hugs. "I'm back for good if you'll have me."

Behind her, Dudley too approached and grabbed his keys from the dresser, a sad smile dancing from his lips.

I pinched my eyes and tightened my hold on Heather. "You are the strongest, most selfless woman I know. If you quit, there is no hope for the rest of us. You can't give up, Heather."

Hastily, I released Heather, eyeing Dudley sliding his feet into his shoes.

She touched my bandaged head gently. "What happened to you?"

"Long story." I cocked my head toward Dudley, but Heather was too busy inspecting me.

He approached her, whispering in her ear. "I'll leave."

"Stay, Dudley." She held his shoulder.

"Yes, stay." I grabbed his other arm.

"I'm not leaving forever and will return. You two have a lot of catching up to do."

"But you just got here." Heather pouted.

"Later, ladybug." He plodded outside with his shoulders slumped.

And my heart broke into pieces.

Heather tugged on my hand and led me to the dining table. "What made you change your mind? Have you forgiven me?"

"A lot of things, but one in particular: I returned looking for roots—a mother, a father, a lover. I tried to help my birth mother with money, but nothing worked."

I pressed on her hand. "And I kept asking myself, 'What would Heather do?' I searched for a mother, and I realized I already had one. Truly. You're the mother I never had. And . . ." I cleared my throat, my voice raspy. "The Lion-Hearted Women of Kapaa is worth preserving. It's a cause that must never die. If there is night, we need light and hope. We'll march forward together, Heather."

She lifted her chin and straightened her back. "We will now that you have returned. But what happened to your head?"

"Another time, okay? Where is Olivia?" I glanced around.

The brightness on Heather's face vanished. "I can't talk about her. Not now."

I nodded, having figured as much. "I'm exhausted and need to put my head down. Do you have a leaky room for me?"

She patted my cheek. "I have a dry one, my dear, your pink room, just the way you left it."

Before leaving for my room, I urged Heather to call Dudley. Unwillingly, she relented. As I dragged my suitcase in, she dialed him on her phone.

Her chatter comforted my ears while I removed my clothes from my suitcase. Suddenly, my eyes began to black out, and I slumped on the bed and pinched shut my eyes, clasping my hands behind my neck. Pain throbbed under the bandage, and I winced. A knock on my door alarmed me, and I wiped my tears, thrusting into my present world. Heather marched inside with a giant strawberry shake and a wide, proud smile.

"You didn't have to."

"Take it." She handed me the glass and sat next to me.

I took a sip. It was so delicious and creamy, I had to close my eyes to savor its taste before placing my hand on Heather's back. "Olivia stole money from you?" I whispered.

Her eyes widened. "Yes, how do you know?"

"It doesn't matter." I shook my head. "We'll find Olivia and Sue."

"Dina warned me. Anyway, she's already flown out of Hawaii. Dudley checked the records." Heather ran her hands through her hair.

"She'll be back." I devoured the rest of the shake.

"How can you be sure?" Heather collected the empty glass from my hands but remained seated.

"I'm sure." I wiped my strawberry mustache.

"How? What do you know that I don't?" She held my knee.

"Heather, marry Dudley." I caressed her hand. "You're taking him for granted! Nobody should take a grain of love in this world for granted. Love is often lost, replaced, and misunderstood. Trust me." I got on my knees and tugged on her hands. "Before I lost my memory, all I wanted was to settle down. Although proud to be independent and self-made, one day I craved quite the opposite—a family with a house and a backyard with two dogs. I don't want the same regret to form in your heart."

Heather's hands flew to her mouth. "Is your memory coming back?"

"It returned in a bolt." My vision blurred as I returned to sitting on the bed.

"Oh my. And yet you came back."

I wiped the moisture from my eye. "I suspect that's why I came back."

"Do you remember Jason?"

"All too well."

"Does that change your stance with him? Tell me everything!" Her eyes filled with tears as she clasped her hands together and leaned forward.

I fluffed a pillow. "We'll not be the only people in the world who love while living apart." My gaze fell on a painting of an Ohia tree on the wall.

"We'll be like the plucked Red Lehua flower and Ohia tree, always together and yet separated."

"You've been reading Hawaii's history? But dear, that is a sorry resolve." She covered her mouth, shaking her head.

"I've bigger fish to fry at the moment." I sighed.

"What is it, dear?" Heather lifted her legs onto the bed, crossing them.

"Olivia, Sue, and other lies people told me—"

"Listen, my dear—"

"I'm not talking about you. You must work on your interfering, but I owe you an apology." I glanced at my hands in my lap. "I now know you didn't take the letters, but you still hid a lot from me, and that must stop."

She licked her lips. "I know. The letters belonged to you, fair and square. But how do you know I didn't take those from you?"

I rose and pulled a paper from my purse, handing it to Heather. "This is a note Sue left for me after she struck me with a fire hydrant."

Heather gasped and opened the note urgently, reading aloud.

Consider this your last chance. Please do nothing stupid, here or in Hawaii. You are safe in bed this time. Next time, I might not be able to save you. I never wanted to harm you, but you threatened my dreams, my life, and my very existence.

I must go to Hawaii to check if you laid a trap for me. Ya, I'm Sue, and I take great pains to avoid the dangers in this world—be it locking my front door three times or hiding your identity. But I can't do this anymore. I had Olivia mail the letters to Jason when he came looking for you. I tried to reunite you two! When I found out he was lying to you, pretending to be Adam, I called and warned you. I only meant to help. You fell on your own, Anna. I never saw it anyway. Let's pray our paths never cross again.
Painfully,
Crazy Sue

Heather and I stared into each other, my heart thumping like the clock that ticked in my pink room. Oh, the months I'd spent here recovering hit me with a vengeance. So much about my life, I hungered to change. So much!

Hiwalani Heather Keahi, the woman who avoided police officers with all her heart and insisted they were up to no good, begged me to open a case reporting Sue. Strange.

But before we finished on Sue, I cautioned her to plan her wedding, as I no longer wished to carry the burden of her life. Heather needed to put relationships first. She scolded me for giving her hypocritical advice. But unlike Jason, Dudley offered his heart and soul without baggage.

After Heather hugged and bid me goodnight, I still couldn't sleep. So I opened my laptop and located my high school yearbook. My finger traced all the names and photos, halting on a boy. I leaned forward running my fingers along his long, silky hair and his dimples that were as prominent then as now.

His body was leaner though, and he wasn't the type I had fancied, but he grew up into a different man—successful, well-built, tall, and so handsome I could cry. Only if I had known. I closed my laptop's lid and fell flat on my bed before climbing out, rushing to my bedroom window, and yanking it open. A steady breeze frisked my hair, and I closed my eyes containing my last fresh memory with Jason in Chicago.

CHAPTER 14 – THE UNWRITTEN AND THE FORGOTTEN

"How important is that that never happened? The words that never were spoken? The feelings that never were shared? Do they matter?"
Mars D. Gill

Only If I Had Known

Chicago O'Hare Airport
August 9, 2013

JASON WAS NOWHERE to be seen in the crowd. Had her last meeting with him passed, denying her a proper goodbye? Anna's hands turned numb. She glanced at her watch and considered following the other passengers to the baggage claim by herself. A familiar hand landed on her shoulder, and her heart fluttered. She turned and melted into him. "I thought you had left." She released him, stroking his unshaven stubble, finding him strikingly more attractive in it.

"I told you I would never leave like that." He caressed her ear. "Sorry, I worried you. It took me a while to get here from the first terminal."

They sauntered toward the baggage claim area, Anna slinking her arm around his waist under his firm embrace. Unrushed, other passengers zipped past them.

"Want to grab something to eat?" he asked when they passed by a deli.

Unable to get the man her heart desired, Anna preferred to hasten their departure, their goodbye a surety like death. "No, the thought of food is nauseating right now." She cleared her throat as they reached the baggage area.

The luggage conveyer belt light triggered the start of the rotation and startled Anna.

She shuddered under his soft grasp, breathing in their last few minutes of togetherness.

"End of a vacation, is it?" a middle-aged man next to them asked.

Jason pulled her into his muscular chest, his Dior perfume etching into her nostrils as he half-smiled at the man. When her bag glided out, Jason retrieved it and sighed deeply, unable to speak louder than a decibel. "Please let me drop you off."

They lumbered away to the escalators.

Certain on not living a life where she had to love secretly, meeting in hotel rooms, ashamed and alone, she brushed his shoulder lovingly and cleared her throat. "I've already ordered my cab from the plane. And besides, your family is waiting for you."

Jason swallowed, resting his forehead against hers while their hug melted into a slow-motion dance. "I don't even have your number." He released her and yanked his phone out from his pocket.

Anna held his hand, shoving the device away. "No phones. No emails. Nothing."

Jason's lower lip fluttered. "Are you serious?"

"We had fun. That's all this was." She shrugged. "You are married and a devoted father—that's who you are."

Anna brushed his shoulder. "I'm leaving you, Jason."

His gaze darted from his shoes to her eyes, his eyelids batting helplessly. "Please—"

"Just hold me."

He drew her into him, his tears wetting her hair.

Wiping her cheeks quickly, she tore herself away. "We must go now," she said, her vision hazy.

He clutched onto her hands until she tore them out. "Please, Anna—"

"Bye, Jason."

"Anna, please don't leave me." His hands hung low as he stepped in her direction.

"Will I get a goodbye?"

A baby cried. Several carts rolled. His chest heaved as he whispered, "Bye."

She turned away from him before he suspended his head and stepped on the escalators, floating down. Anna wiped her tears, exiting through the double doors.

When the breeze hit her body, she jerked around, stealing one last glance at him. Descending, his eyes affixed on her. Meeting her gaze, they widened, and he struggled as though climbing back up. She wiped her tears and dashed toward the cab lane where her ride waited and hurled her bag in its trunk, climbing inside, her heart fluttering.

As they eased out behind the bumper-to-bumper traffic, Anna broke down. She heaved and sobbed like a child. The driver glanced at her in the rearview mirror, opening his mouth but asking nothing.

Then two thuds jolted the slow-moving cab. Jason! He peered inside, the cab screeching to a halt.

"What do you want me to do?" the driver asked.

"Drive!"

The cab sped off as Jason dashed behind it until his frame became smaller and smaller, disappearing behind the bend.

CHAPTER 15 – THE FIGHT

"Love is a madness; if thwarted it develops fast."
Mark Twain

The Lover Who Never Left

Hawaii
Present Day

ON MY WAY to the local hospital, I drummed my fingers on the steering wheel while waiting for the traffic light to turn green. The CT scans lay next to me on the passenger's seat, and the afternoon sun soaked everything in bright light.

It was then my gaze fell on Jason standing at the crosswalk. Without a second thought, I ejected out of my running car and marched to him, placing my hand on his shoulder. "Jason!"

It wasn't him.

Under the stranger's glare, my mouth fell, and I trudged back to my car. A driver behind me honked and yelled, "Move!"

Another person, a young man with long hair, behind him extended his thumb and pinky finger. "Aloha, my man, aloha. Patience."

Shivering, I steered away, shaking my head. I should have returned to Jason at Chicago, and all this could have been avoided. Why did I write those letters instead? Maybe it was the old-fashioned ideas I had about marriage and the surety of happiness. I was naïve. For the rest of the drive, I ignored everything except the road in front.

When I climbed atop the elevator to Dr. Lee's office, I glanced away from every face in my way.

I didn't want to see him in everyone.

Soon, I sat across Dr. Lee, the same doctor who had nursed me to health after my memory loss. No longer a resident but a director now, he scratched his neck. "How did your memory return?"

I adjusted myself in my seat and smiled. "I walked into a fire hydrant."

He dropped my file and burst out laughing. "Well, that's safer than the last accident." He picked up the paperwork and lifted a sheet, percolating in his thoughts before glancing at me. "Sometimes only trauma can erase another trauma. Ms. Everly, your CT scan is healthy." He beamed.

I sighed in relief, the turbulent memory of the stranger yelling at me at the traffic signal fresh inside my mind. But I was healthy.

Soon, I checked out and stood in front of the elevators, tapping my foot.

A man in a suit and tie emerged from the adjoining mental ward before I stared right into his eyes, forcing him to drop his eyelids and take three steps away with crossed arms. I hung my head and pinched shut my eyes before shoving my hand in my purse, feeling for my car keys. I was done searching for him, done, done, done—no more gawking at men. The elevator doors dinged and parted, and I opened my eyes.

My keys fell from my fingers as a man wearing a sweater-vest over blue-collared shirt emerged. While I had no intention to enter with the uncomfortable man in his late forties who still had his arms crossed, I purposefully evaded my gaze from the new guy too. Picking up the fallen keys, the person who had come out had frozen over me.

I jerked my head and flipped my hand. "Do you need anything?" My keys dropped again.

His cheeks dipped hollow where dimples once beamed. A faint stubble lined his jaw, but that kindness in his eyes was ancient. My eyes welled up, disbelieving that I glanced into Jason's blue eyes for real. Desperate but unable to bridge the distance, I stood at arm's length.

"Are you hurt?" He pointed to my head.

I gulped and stared at my feet. "Long story." I glanced behind him at the mental ward, the only other unit besides trauma.

A doctor in blue scrubs and white coat waited.

I cleared my throat. "What about you?"

"Long story, too." He smiled.

My heart sank when my gaze traveled to the floral bag hung from his shoulder, the one with my letters.

Catching my stare, he whispered, "I still read them, Anna."

The doctor in blue scrubs and a white coat tapped on his shoulder. "We're ready for you, Mr. Barnes."

A deep, poignant worry compressed my heart into a ball.

"I have to get going. My number hasn't changed." He made the telephone sign with his hands to his ears. "Call me?"

He followed the doctor and I behind them. While Jason disappeared inside the double doors and into another room, a man sat in a wheelchair, gazing straight ahead. I swallowed and pressed the elevator button as a wild shriek tore through the air, and I shuddered. Somewhere in the middle of that chaotic ward roamed Jason Barnes, hiding an ocean inside him.

I flung open the door of the villa. "Guess who I saw today!"

Dudley jumped in his seat.

"Sorry, I didn't mean to startle you. Where is your better half?" I tossed my keys on the dresser.

"Not here. I've been waiting for two hours now." He held up his cell phone. "She won't answer my calls either. Wasn't she with you?"

My breathing hastened while my voice turned shrill. "No. Very unlike her." I leaned on the dresser. "She didn't tell me she had errands, and in fact, I had her car."

Dudley bolted out of his seat. "We should search for her."

I nodded.

We grabbed our coats and headed into town. We visited the restaurants where she conducted her meetings, the shops she frequented, her friends' homes. But she'd vanished into the thin air.

When I pulled into a police station that night, Dudley's face reddened.

His eyes widened. "Are you sure you want to involve the police? Heather's opinions about them are black and white."

I turned off the car. "Rather, I should have listened to Heather and done this sooner." My throat ached as I stormed out, Dudley following close behind.

At the entrance of the mud-colored building, Dudley grabbed my arms and whispered into my ear. "What haven't you told me?"

I hung my head, and my lip quivered. "I brought trouble with me. Let's go, and you'll hear the rest."

The big, tan cop's belly fluttered while laughing. "Attempted murder. Kidnapping. Obstruction of justice and theft. Are we writing a soap opera?"

Dudley, too, glared at me before whispering, "What's this got to do with Heather?"

I leaned in toward the police officer and clenched my teeth. "Sue Miller attempted to kill me. Twice. I saved her note where she threatened me."

He gestured for the note. "Show it to me."

I tugged on my dry throat. "I can bring it from home, but that's beside the point. Heather, the founder of Lion-Hearted Women of Kapaa, is missing."

"Heather? You mean Hiwalani Keahi?"

I shifted in my chair. "Yes. Do you know her?"

"Very well. She's a big, strong woman. How long has she been missing?" He wrote in his notebook.

"Since this afternoon."

He glanced up with a smirk and then cocked at another officer sitting at an adjoining table. "Just this afternoon, ma'am? Give her some time to return. Why do you worry about only one afternoon?" He scratched his protruding belly. "And I doubt Ms. Miller is involved."

I leaned far forward, threatening to fall off my chair. "Sue and her partner Olivia stole from Heather before they hurt me in Chicago." I pointed to my head. "But—"

"Woah. Wait, wait, wait. In Chicago?"

"Yes."

"You know what I think, Ms. . . ."

"Everly."

"Ms. Everly, there is nothing I can do about this situation. Sue Miller tried to kill you. You escaped. Right? Did you file a police report in Chicago when it happened?"

"No, I came here. The longer I stayed there, the longer I was in danger."

Dudley shook his head and leaned back into his chair.

I hadn't even told the officer about Sue's connection to my memory loss, and he'd already discredited my story as a concoction of my overactive my mind.

"Next time you are in danger, Ms. Everly, I'd advise you to go to the nearest police station instead of the farthest one." The officer at the adjacent table guffawed.

I scowled at them. Heather was right to despise the police. While Dudley compressed his hands into fists, I pulled out my phone from my pocket, but no news of Heather was there either.

The police officer continued. "Listen, Heather's a strong woman. I'm sure she's fine. Go home and wait for her till the morning."

"What about Sue Miller and her partner?"

"It's out of my jurisdiction."

"Listen, a year and a half ago, I lost my memory right here in Hawaii, and Heather saved my life." I flung my finger at them. "Sue was my coworker and the only person who witnessed my accident. She never revealed my identity to Heather, and I demand she be investigated."

"Hire a detective."

"What?"

"Get some evidence. It's too late to open a case that old based solely on your word. Come back when you have something concrete."

"If anything happens to Heather as you sit and joke, I'll take you to the court!" Dudley punched the table.

The officer rose. "Listen here! We are honorable, reasonable men. I'll file a missing person's report for Hiwalani if that makes you feel better. But I doubt anything comes of it."

Close to midnight, Dudley and I entered an empty home, alone and dejected, disappearing into our respective bedrooms without uttering a word. With the door closed, I texted Jason: *I miss you. Why didn't you call me?*

I slumped onto my bed. Tears overwhelmed me, and my tired eyelids closed. When they opened, I couldn't remember my whereabouts at first. Panicked by the feeling, I hopped out of bed. My pink room came into view. I sighed and grabbed my phone. Heather's absence had drained my soul.

I crept out into the living room, where Dudley snored with one leg dangling over the couch.

I rubbed my eyes. Twenty-nine unread messages from Jason flashed across my phone's screen. Everything from "How are you?" and "So nice to see you again," to "Want to jog on our usual trail?" Yet no answer to my question.

I slipped into my flip-flops and threw a thin fleece over me.

The sun had yet to rise. I quietly closed the door behind me and jogged to the bike path. Far away on the eastern horizon, the sun barely crept above the ocean, not yet gracing the mountains of Hawaii. I hugged myself. Dampness coated the bike path as I carefully veered north toward downtown Kapaa. The waves slathered and rumbled in gentle crests. I tugged my phone close to my chest, awaiting the world's call to shatter my loneliness. But nothing.

When I reached the town, the orange sun illuminated the outskirts of the coast, everything still asleep, and I settled my gaze on the giant lock on Mrs. Parker's antique shop. Rustling from the side of the building distracted me. A thin, athletic woman shoved trash in a large bin. Birds chirped their morning orchestra, and she turned, revealing her familiar, freckled face, and I gasped. But just as quickly, she marched in the opposite direction.

A biting ache seared my chest. How could she not acknowledge me? My smile drowned in shame. "Hey!" I shouted, dashing after her.

She jerked ten feet away before hastening.

"Hey, Desiree!" With no intention of losing her again, I sped up. "Why are you running from me?!"

When I reached the corner she had disappeared into, a sharpshooting head blow blinded me. I screamed, sinking to the ground, gritting my teeth, my head in my hands.

A strong pair of hands grabbed my shoulders, and I lifted my head. Jason!

"You have a knack for danger." Worry laced his unflinching eyes. "It's a good thing I saw you on the bike trail. Let's get you out of danger."

He lifted me off my feet and carried me along the bike trail, his warm breaths soothing my head and calming my heart. At the villa, he put me in his pickup truck's passenger seat, harnessed me in a seatbelt like a child, and drove away. I asked him nothing about where we were going. I hungered to be taken by him, shutting my eyes and drifting away into sleep.

The waves foamed and crashed. We sat at the Beachside restaurant, a place Heather frequented to conduct therapy sessions with the girls.

I pressed on his hands, a steady pain reverberating my head. "I now remember that I didn't come to Hawaii to sightsee or get over you. After months of mourning her death, unusual Twitter feeds on her account had driven me here to investigate." I wiped a tear, my eyelids fluttering and voice heavy. "Right now, we need to find Heather. She's strong, but after Sue attacked me—"

He released his hand, slamming his fist on the table. "Sorry, that woman was up to no good. Are you sure Sue could take on Heather?"

I frowned. "I'm not sure of anything anymore. My accident is hazy although I'm remembering the rest of my life now. But I saw Isabella and Sue together—they seemed close."

Jason furrowed his brow, sipping his coffee before our server brought our meals. I waited, but not a reaction escaped his lips. When the server receded, I bit into my taro bagel, the rising sun casting its beams on our faces.

Jason dug into his Loco Moco. "Isabella is harmless."

I dropped my bagel, curling my fingers into a fist. Heather had told me how Isabella had hurt him with false accusations, and yet he backed her. I shook my head. "B—"

He grabbed my hands. "Listen, first things first— Heather. We can put up her posters across the island. That's easy. She's a well-known person, thanks to her social involvement. Second, stay away from Desiree and Mrs. Parker."

I freed my hands and leaned back. "Jason, how can you ask me to do that? Mrs. Parker called me, by the way, to say that you have been bothering her for information. What was that all about?"

Same old smile. I pursed my lips, disallowing his charm to melt my fury.

Wiping his lips with his napkin, he raised his brow. "Desiree and Mrs. Parker are trouble. I've been on their trail ever since you left. And—"

"What is it you know?"

He picked up his phone. "One problem at a time," he said, dialing a number and holding it up to his ear. "Yes, hello. Is this the *ChicagoGoers* magazine? Yes. Please connect me to Mr. Brady."

Ian Brady was my boss.

"Hi, Ian. Thank goodness you're free to talk. Have you heard from Sue Miller?" He pressed his temples. "Just as I suspected. Thanks. No, that'll be unnecessary."

"You are a well-connected man," I commented when he hung up.

"Let's count ourselves lucky for that then. As I suspected, she's no longer with the company." He threw cash on the table and rose. "And if I remember her correctly, she's not stupid enough to follow you to Hawaii with her real name. I have an idea."

I rose and followed him outside, struggling to keep up, my throbbing head in my hands. "What idea? Do you think Isa—"

He halted and grabbed my shoulders, his kind eyes sparkling. "Anna, focus on one problem at a time, okay?"

Sunlight assaulted our eyes when we pulled into the villa and marched inside.

As we removed our shoes at the entrance, Dudley rushed from room to room, throwing his belongings into a suitcase.

I froze. "Where are you going?!"

"Back to Honolulu." He flipped the lid, zipping it.

My hand flew to my heart, tears pricking my eyes. "Why?"

He toddled to me with his bag and bowed to Jason. "Hello, young man."

Nodding his head, Jason backed away from us and the door.

I shifted from foot to foot. "But we need you here! We brought flyers to hang. We—"

"Anna, my sweetheart." He let go his suitcase and stroked my cheek. "I'm not worried about Heather one bit. That woman knows how to take care of herself and others." He dropped his hand and sighed. "I sincerely believe that she has set up this facade to leave me."

I clutched his shoulders. "Listen, Heather is awful at communication. I can say that from personal experience. But she is the most selfless person I know. She only tries too hard, and she loves you."

He released my hands, lifted his bag, and strode around me. "She's not in trouble. Trust me."

"But what if she is?" I flew to the door, blocking his exit.

"I don't feel it, my dear." He pulled out a piece of paper from his pocket and placed it on the palm of my hand. "This is from her."

I unfolded it with trembling hands. In her childish handwriting, she wrote:

December 6, 2014
Dudley, my love, don't wait up for me. I have important business to handle.
Heather

Dudley nodded and yanked open the door that creaked ominously.

My voice came out heavy and jittery. "This is from yesterday, Dudley. She meant to say don't wait for dinner. Today is a new day, and she hasn't returned."

"I know." He kissed my forehead and left, the breeze flinging the loose short around his back.

Sure, Heather had demons from her childhood abuse. And she'd spent her entire life erasing that stain, but somehow, the scars kept redrawing.

"Dudley may have a point," Jason said.

I stared through the open door, holding back tears. "She would call me."

He pulled me into a hug and rubbed my back. "Anna, this island is packed with Heather's friends."

"You're simplifying her life." I swallowed, tearing myself from him. "Where there are friends, there are enemies." I shut the door, grabbed my gold necklace, and shoved it in my mouth, avoiding biting my nails that had no room left for shortening.

At the same moment, Jason's phone rang. He glanced at it and slid his feet in his shoes.

"Where are you going?"

"I'm sorry, but I forgot I had an important deadline. I'll be back."

"Jason, plea—"

The door slammed before my words could reach his ears. I dropped on the ground. The villa that once bubbled with women, rang with Heather's laughter, was now haunted by cold emptiness.

The long drive was supposed to clear my head. It wasn't supposed to go like this: Panting for breath, swerving into the parking lot of the police station, climbing out without shutting my door and storming into the mud-colored building where Sergeant Lewis rose with a file in his hands. He dropped it on the table and marched across to me as I clutched my chest, gasping for breath. "I f-f-found . . ."

He shushed me and pulled around a chair, gesturing to it. "Ms. Everly, please calm yourself. Here. Take a seat. Tom, please get Ms. Everly water."

I shook my head. "I don't need any. I found . . ."

"I found something too. Who should go first?"

I pointed at him holding my parched throat unable to speak a syllable, slumping low into the chair. Better him first.

His colleague brought a cup of water, and Sergeant Lewis yanked it into my hands. "You need this, Ms. Everly. This is important, and pay close attention to every word I say. Do you understand?"

"What is it?"

"Please drink the water." He pulled a chair and sat right next to me.

"I don—"

"Miss, drink." He leaned forward, his unblinking eyes narrowing.

Not believing he was the same man who had laughed at me the previous night, I gulped it down in one big swoop and handed the glass back.

He slammed it on the table and cleared his throat. "Okay. After you left last night, I tracked down Sue Miller." He leaned back.

"And?"

"She and her partner turned themselves into the police."

"What?" I jumped out of my seat.

"Sit, please," he whispered coarsely, and I shot into my seat, gripping the armrests.

He grasped my armrest too. "I called my friend who works for the station at River North, and he checked on Ms. Miller's files. Because she pleaded guilty to attempting to harm you and then saving your life—are you listening, Ms. Everly?" He leaned so forward that his breath fell on my hands clasping my chair's armrests.

I released the chair, leaned far back, and clutched the locket around my neck, boggling straight ahead. "Y-yes, I am."

"Because she turned herself in and her account matched your charges, she will face a lenient penalty like rehab." He scratched his beard, shaking his head. "In other words, Ms. Miller and her partner, your prime suspect in Hiwalani's disappearance, are in the clear and probably still in Chicago. Are you still with me?"

I nodded.

He arched his brows, his hands clasping into his lap "Ma'am, are you sure Hiwalani is not being Hiwalani?"

"What do you mean?" My eyes welled up, tears spilling over.

"She has no enemies on the island, and people love her for all she has given back through the Lion-Hearted Women of Kapaa. Perhaps taking care of similar business?" He brought his chin to his neck, glancing at me from above his glasses.

"B-but . . . her phone."

"What about it?"

"I found it dead at the villa." I pulled out her chilly device. "If she's so loved on the island of Kauai, is there no one's phone she could use to assure us she's okay?"

His eyes widened, and he cleared his throat. "That's strange, indeed. Do you have any other suspicions?"

"No."

CHAPTER 16 – FINDING THE TRUTH

*"A lie can travel halfway around the world while the truth
is putting on its shoe."*
Mark Twain

Jason

The Hidden Antique Shop
Same Day

JASON STARED at the lights twinkling along the mountainside, his hands stiff, his black suit impeccable. When the door rattled and footsteps entered the hotel room, his face hung low, but he didn't turn.

She slinked up to him, and in a drunken, raspy voice whispered, "Mr. Barnes, your present is here."

He tensed, and a smile barely flickered from his face as she, in black lace lingerie, glided to the TV, flipping it on to an audio channel playing sensual music.

She gestured to the sofa, and he strolled to it, his hands in his pocket.

Joining him there, she crouched next to him, loosening his thin black tie. "You sure have dashing style, Mr. Barnes."

He smiled, trying to suppress the lump building in his throat. "Thank you, Dimples," he said and slumped into the sofa. He'd had just enough time to shave his beard, wanting to look proper for his mission. As soon as she unbuttoned his shirt, he grabbed her hand. "What's the rush? Let's talk."

"Talk?" Her lips quivered.

He smirked and leaned back. "Yeah, ease into it."

She cleared her throat and adjusted a few strands of her obviously fake blond hair behind her ear. "Are you nervous?"

"I've never done this before." His gaze didn't tear from her face.

Her lips moved forcing a smile, but the stiffness in her body gave away her discomfort. "Okay. You can talk. I only ask questions." She adjusted herself next to him and crossed her arms.

"Sure. Fire away."

"Do you enjoy being a police officer?" She brushed the dust off his shoulder as he chuckled.

"*Eh*, it's okay."

She tilted her head. "How come you've never done this before?"

"My marriage just broke."

She twisted her lips, glancing around. "Listen, I'm not the Pretty Woman type of gal. You can pay me if you don't want to do me."

"Payment was for sex." He held her arm so tightly, her color paled.

"Get on—"

"Desiree Darlington." He leaned in and brought his face close to hers as her eyes widened.

She struggled, trying to break from his hold. "Who are you, and what do you want from me? My name is—"

"Dimples, I know. But I'm not here about that."

Her gaze flashed toward the door.

"I'm here about Anna Everly. Remember her?"

She broke free and gathered her belongings.

Jason rose. "Fine, fine, leave. It's in your best interest to not tell Mrs. Parker though."

She stopped short. "And why's that?"

"Rather, why would you shun your best friend and chose this life? We can get you out."

She slung her giant purse over her shoulder and dashed to the door, and Jason followed. "Here's my business card." He slid it into her purse. "If you change your mind."

"I won't." She shuddered before slamming the door shut.

Home Without Heather

The Villa, Kapaa, HI
Midnight, Present Day

FLASHED ACROSS my phone's screen: *Are you at home?*

Jason.

My trembling fingers responded with a *yes*. Next, I typed: "*Jason, I need to*" and hit backspace, typing instead: "*How is Isa.*" Deleted again. Moisture clung to my lashes as my fingers played tug of war with unsent texts

I sat upright and lifted my chin, typing with a new resolution, asking him why he still read my letters when the doorbell rang, and my phone slipped from beneath my fingers.

I dashed to the door, picturing Heather's smile. But it was him. Still, I welcomed him, burying myself in his warm embrace.

He planted a long kiss on my cheek. "Are you okay, my darling?"

I wiped my tears and tore from his arms. "I have so many questions."

"I do too. Want to go for a walk?"

"It's dark and breezy."

"Perfect weather." He rubbed my shoulder.

I smiled, grabbed my pink raincoat, and slipped into my shoes. Outside, a family sat around the resort's table with a firepit near the beach.

Surrounded by dancing tiki torches, we strolled to the bike trail, where the roaring waves and the rustling palm trees orchestrated a symphony.

"Now that you remember everything, are you still mine?" he asked, grabbing my hand.

I was his from the first time I'd laid eyes on him at the conference. "I should ask you the same, as I don't have a spouse or children. You do"

"I've separated from Isabella."

"In spirit?"

"And on paper. She moved on quite easily, dating online, and I—"

"You what?" I halted.

"I kept rereading your letters for more clues." He pressed on my hand and resumed strolling, the waves roaring louder with the wind. A biker whirred around us, and far away a dog barked.

"Why?" I swallowed.

He caressed my hand. "Your words drenched in heartache that spoke of your love—how in the world could you leave so easily after writing them?"

Dudley's frame carrying his suitcase to the car came to mind. He too had slipped away effortlessly. Did he cry into his pillow right now? Write letters?

Jason drew me closer, and I rested my head on his shoulder. "Sometimes we're closest to the people we're farthest from, but if you'll have me—"

He halted and squeezed my hands. "I'll give you a million better reasons to write me letters." His chest heaved as he shoved my hair off my face. And my lips sank into his, his hands sliding under my shirt to my waist.

The next morning, he buried his face into a pillow, his chest moving rhythmically, his steady breaths humming. At night, he'd crashed on my bed immediately after returning from our midnight walk. I rested my head on my palm, watching him sleep before I flopped my legs off the bed. As soon as my toes touched the ground, his breaths hastened. His face shook, and his fists clenched. "No!" he yelled. "No, no!"

I stroked his hair and planted pecks on his face.

He jolted awake, panting for breath, his blue eyes resembling earth.

I firmly embraced his jittering body, patting his back. "It's okay. It was just a dream. Do you want to talk about it?"

I hadn't seen this side of Jason, not even as Adam. He was the strong one, always helping others.

When he yanked himself out of my grasp, I straightened, crossing my legs.

He scratched his forehead, glancing around before whispering, "My mom." He slumped on the pillow, holding his head.

"It's okay if—"

He clutched my hand. "No, I want to." His eyes glistened while he stared at the ceiling. "She used to be the happiest, most cheerful person in my life." He swallowed. "Within the year after my father left us, on my fourteenth birthday, they sent me to my distant uncle's home."

"Why?"

He clasped his hands. "Sh-she lost her mind."

I uncrossed my legs and folded them underneath me, my eyelids flickering. "The other day at the hospital?"

"I wish I was visiting her." He sighed, rising and yanking the pillow onto his lap.

"A week after they took her, my mother called me, begging me to get her out. I had no money. That weekend . . ." He threw the pillow across the room.

"What happened?" I touched his shoulder, but he pushed me away as I covered my mouth.

"I'm sorry." He clenched my shoulder, pleading with helpless eyes before turning away from me. "I brought her flowers, but she'd hung herself."

Tears flowed down my cheeks. I grabbed him, rocking together.

He tightened his hold on me. "I can't help but compare all hospitals to the place in which my mother killed herself. Am I going insane? I'm so freaking alone that I fear I'll end up in one!"

Jason and alone? Not in my lifetime.

That afternoon, Dina arrived with an army of women.

"We found these flyers." One held up a familiar paper with Heather's smiling picture. "Can we help?"

A petite girl stepped forward, tucking her hair behind her ear. "Heather saved me from my abusive husband. What can I do?"

When Jason emerged out of the bedroom, he froze scanning the bustling living room. I bounced my eyebrows at him setting a bowl of apples on the kitchen counter as he reached me, kissing me passionately. My cheeks burned while Dina smirked on the sidelines.

His breaths melted on my face while he ran his hand through my hair and asked, "Do you feel differently about Desiree now that you remember?

Setting his hands aside and clasping mine across my chest, I frowned, upset at the choice of his topic. "What do you mean?"

Jason grabbed an apple. "Well, what do you remember other than your nightmares?"

I nodded at Heather's friends sitting on the couch. "I used to be the roadblock keeping her from ill-informed choices. She probably found her freedom in Hawaii." I sighed. "Desiree has willfully forgotten me. She didn't hunger for a childhood friend like I did." A lump enlarged in my throat.

"Hmm." He crunched his apple. "Why would you dream about her despite losing your memory if your bond was that shallow?"

My stomach knotted. Guilt. That's why. When I wanted a married man, I drowned in regret for judging Desiree. If I never realized her shallowness, I would have carried the burden of driving her away.

He waved his hand at my face. "Anna? You okay?"

I turned and held his face. "I don't know why. Maybe there's a greater purpose to this."

"It's Desiree's business," he mumbled through a mouthful of apple. "At all online portals, the shop belongs to Desiree, not Mrs. Parker, and yet Mrs. Parker lied about her death. Desiree may carry a bigger stake in this than we thought." Jason pulled me, leading me to my bedroom.

"Where are you taking me?"

"I need to show you something in private." He locked the bedroom door and yanked a camera out of his bag. Tossing his eaten apple in the garbage, he slid through photos.

I snatched it out of his hand and gaped.

The first: a sexy blonde girl in lingerie kissed his cheek with her hand on his tie.

Second: they sat together—him and Desiree.

I slumped on the bed. "Wait—" My eyes bulged. "How—where—what?"

He held up his hands. "Don't be angry. I visited the shop last night to investigate, and being a man looking for sex was the only way into the ring. I hid the camera on a timer to capture proof."

I glared at him. "You had—"

"No! God, no. I left a card with her in case she wanted to get out of that place."

I shook my head. Increasingly, the world turned out to be shallow and fake.

He grabbed my shoulder before whispering, "There's more. I saw Heather's name on a roster stuck on a wooden board by the front desk."

"What?! And you tell me this now?" I jumped off the bed. "What does that mean for Heather?"

"She paid them a visit the day she disappeared."

I clutched my head while Dina's voice became audible through the shut door. What was I supposed to do? Shout for everyone to stop searching? "Are you sure you saw Heather's name?"

"I'm sure."

"Did you investigate further?"

"Desire knew my identity by then and had the guards escorting me out."

The outside bell rang, and I shuddered.

Stroking my chest, I followed him to the living room where Dina yanked the door open.

We both froze.

A police officer greeted her, and they spoke for a moment before Dina turned toward me for a minute. My heart raced, but her face gave nothing away.

Jason tucked a strand of my hair behind my ear and whispered, "I think Heather's going after the cops—"

I faced him, my eyes widening.

He continued. "I had to pretend to be a police officer. Hawaii's law allows prostitution for cops."

"That's absurd! Heather wouldn't stand by that."

Dina nodded at the officer, and I swallowed hard. "Besides, she could have done that from here."

He shook his head. "I don't understand either why Heather didn't expose the ring from here."

Just then, Dina collapsed, and the officer caught her in his arms.

We rushed to the door as I pulled Dina away, cradling her face.

Jason rubbed his mouth and crossed his arms. "What happened, sir?"

"We found Heather's body washed ashore on the North Beach. I'm sorry."

The Funeral

Kapaa, HI
December 2014

RAIN PATTERED the black umbrellas over our heads as the priest sang a fitting tribute in the local language.

The cause of Heather's death was listed as drowning on her death certificate. The media headlines called it a suicide. But we knew it was murder.

Strangers collected around us. Like me, Heather had no family—even her uncle was dead. She and I had that in common, and we filled each other's voids up until now. But Heather's hole had been filled with kindness. As evidence, the world Heather had befriended descended to her funeral today.

Thankful for his warm embrace, I clung onto Jason, staring at the water droplets on my black shoes, the priest's moving lips, the wreath on the closed casket—anywhere but at Dudley, who stood by the casket. He should have fought for Heather and joined our search. Now his tears were useless. Heather died because love had left her side.

Her memorial service ran hours. My voice had fled, but I didn't need it today.

The infinite stories shared by the women Heather had enriched filled the quietness.

Sue and Olivia sat in the back row, wiping tears.

When they came up front to talk to Dina, Sue's stare on Jason's hands clasping mine burned.

Dudley, too, approached us apologizing profusely for leaving. I assured him with empty words: "It's all right." "No worries," I said. What I really meant was "buzz off." He trudged back to his car in the rain before taking off down the road.

In silence, Jason and I lumbered back to the villa along with the girls who had volunteered.

At the villa, we filled our coffee mugs and huddled on the couch. The girls discussed Lion-Hearted Women of Kapaa's future with apprehension. They slumped far into their seats. Dina held her head. Another wiped incessant tears. For them, Heather's work died with her. I glanced from face to face.

My heart full, a sense of urgency overtook me, and I rose with my coffee in hand.

Jason leaned forward in his seat.

"It's not over!" I boomed, setting my mug on the table. "This is just the beginning, and I intend to continue Heather's causes." I held up a finger. "She was last seen at the invisible ring protected by the police, and I plan to investigate what happened to her. She didn't die in vain. Who is with me?"

Dina cheered.

"Heather would have done the same for any of us, and if we unite, for as long as we exist, Lion-Hearted Women of Kapaa will remain."

The women rose, clapped, and roared. We hugged and wiped our tears. Our plans fluttered out of our mouths like busy bees, and we took notes, as we were Heather now.

A tropical storm battered the island that evening. It rumbled, rain slapping the windows. Broken branches littered the beaches. Amid all the noise, the bell rang.

All of us were here. I sat upright as Dina marched to the door.

Maybe Heather would just waltz in and wake us from this nightmare.

Foolish thought.

Outside the door, drenched in rain while sobbing and trembling, stood Isabella.

Jason sprang to his feet and rushed to her side, and my heart convulsed in a painful spasm.

Isabella sank in his embrace, weeping like a child. The wound from Heather's loss opened again, and I bled inside out. Despite the gut-wrenching pain, I breathed deeply and fetched a glass of water for her. After two towels and a cup of hot cocoa, a beverage Heather had offered to all ailing people who sought her help, Isabella calmed. Not once did she look me in the eye.

Everyone stepped back but stared at her, sitting in the chair with him kneeling and holding her hand.

She wiped a tear. "Henry broke up with me."

He pressed down on her hands. "I'm sorry."

"He had a problem with the kids. Too much responsibility. I have no other place to go," she wheezed.

His color paled. "The kids?"

"They're at my parents'."

As Jason's face crunched, I shook my head. How had she found him at the villa?

The girls whispered wondering who she was, whose pain outweighed the one contained in our hearts.

Her hands squeezed Jason's, and I glanced away. With Heather's untimely death and the threat of losing Jason over again, my purpose for returning to Hawaii disintegrated before my eyes. Ashes.

Dina patted my back, her creased forehead spelling her concern for me. Isabella brought unwanted answers to my questions.

Witnessing his concern for his ex-wife, who had plotted with Sue against me, was uncomfortable beyond words. Why didn't he care how much her presence hurt me? Someone pulled Dina aside, and I quietly slipped into my room, glared into the mirror and slapped my face. "Fool!"

I wandered, shuttling between Chicago and Hawaii like an unwanted comma, an insignificant cough.

With my head in my hands, I slumped on my bed.

The clock's ticktock reminded me of my time at the hospital, aching, longing for an unknown commodity. Memoryless and full of pain.

I concentrated on its echoes.

As the crowd lessened, furthering Heather's cause became the anthem of my life. So what if I had no clue what I was doing? I had blogged on every topic dear to Heather except the final one that'd cost her life. Nonetheless, I tried. I wrote: "Heather's death couldn't be a suicide. Neither would she tolerate the exploitation of women."

As I typed on my computer on the dining table, the bell rang, and I scuttled to the front door.

After I flung it open, my gaze fell on a large package placed on the ground. A UPS truck pulled away from the driveway before I lifted it. It wasn't heavy compared to its size.

Inside at the dining table, I yanked its tape off. "Dina. Dina!" I shouted.

She came charging out of her room. "What's wrong?"

I shifted on my feet. "I got a package from Heather."

Her jaw dropped. "Posthumously?"

We stared at each other before she rushed to me.

We ripped and ripped, letting the paper cut our fingers. Out came a pile of documents we split between ourselves. My heart leaped to my throat as I read one, sitting down on a chair.

The ring! The documents exposed the secret business behind the antique shop run by dead people, employing thousands of employees. Worse, it catered to a large police population.

I tapped my finger on a pile of papers, rearing my head above the documents. "This was Heather's final purpose."

"Yes, but . . ." Dina scratched her chin. "You can't trust the police with this."

"Of course, not."

I rose and paced, my hands clasped. "But I'll write about it, give interviews, and finish what Heather couldn't."

Dina clenched her fists, leaning back in her chair. "But it's dangerous. Heather lost her life. We know she didn't commit suicide."

"Right, and that's why we must finish it." I halted and grabbed Dina's shoulders, peering into her brown eyes.

She cleared her throat and whispered, "This is about your friend Desiree."

My hands grew numb and dropped into Dina's hands.

I stared at my feet. Desiree! What kind of person faked death and refused to recognize her friend in need all because of some filthy business?

"It's okay." I patted her shoulder and dashed inside my bedroom.

The package added fuel to my mission. The autopsy results showed she died within hours of being found, two days after going missing.

So she had to have spent little time at the ring to get to this information. Was she hiding there? How had she gotten past security?

I sprang back into the living room. Dina wasn't there. Shoving the papers back into its cardboard box, I headed out with it to photocopy all the important documents—the deed of Desiree's business, the photos, etc. and deposited the originals in a bank.

A war had begun.

I dreamed nightly about Heather marching inside a burning city, her baseball bat in her hand, her dashing into the blaze and disappearing. A pool of sweat awoke me daily in this manner. Today too I spent extra-long in the shower, erasing the memory of the nightmare before leaving for the supermarket. When I returned rounding the corner into our driveway, sun sparkled through every nook and cranny, and someone waited in the porch. Desiree!

She tapped her pencil heel, hiding under a royal hat over her head. Heavy makeup. Perfect figure. No, not the same person I'd met at the garbage bin with the disheveled hair. She was at work today. I emerged from the car, hiding a tiny tremor as she fixed her gaze on me.

"Hi," she said when I was at arm's length.

"What do you want?"

She cleared her throat. "Can I come in?"

"What for?" I tightened the grip on my purse.

"I came to talk to you." She crossed her arms.

"You recognize me now?" My brows lifted.

While she laughed it off, I unlocked the villa and stepped aside.

She, an unworthy soul, entered our safe house.

I pouted and sat across from her while she adjusted herself on the couch, repeatedly.

"I know you very well, Anna. I'm sorry I couldn't help you. And now Heather—so tragic." She shut her eyes.

"Cut the crap, all right?" I lifted my hand.

"Right. Nothing is free in life, and we must pay a price for everything." She lifted her chin, her red lips shimmering. "Though I had to sever ties with my past, I'm content. It's a dangerous business. Helplessness forced me on this course, but it's the best thing to have happened to me."

I smirked. "Why are you facing your past now?"

She switched her crossed leg. "Keep the judgments to yourself. I don't want to hear about your disapproval, contempt, or anything else."

"We're near strangers."

"Sad as that is, I'm here with a specific agenda."

"And what's that?"

She unfolded her legs, leaned forward, and brought her fingertips together. "First, I've never judged you or anybody on their life choices. By assuming a new identity, I've paid the price for my life. Or else I would have ended up behind bars long ago." Her lips twisted into a smile. "Just because my thriving business doesn't sit well with this nation's laws doesn't mean they should deprive me of my livelihood." She shook her head. "Your articles are so unfair! You're negating the experts by claiming—"

"We both know she didn't kill herself!" I leaned forward and clenched my teeth.

"That's what the experts are saying. Nonetheless, I wish you no harm and hope you'll stay out of my way." She grabbed her purse and slid it on her shoulders.

I leaned back. "Or else what? I'll walk into the ocean and kill myself too?"

She shook her head and chuckled, rising. "Anna, I may have changed my name, but that doesn't make me a murderer."

"My life's mission is to avenge Heather's death." I rose and glared into her eyes, crossing my arms.

A slight shiver flashed on her face.

"I expect nothing but judgment from you. Do this as a favor to me, for old time's sake. Let me be. This is all I have." With her sunglasses on, she sashayed to the door and reached for the knob. "It's a dangerous but limitless business. We do well because there's a need for us." She faced me, still holding the door. "I don't want to see you hurt."

I tightened my arms across my chest. "Just say it, Desiree. What would happen?"

"I don't wish to see you get hurt." She shook her head and slammed the door shut on my face.

I scoffed. Challenge accepted!

I picked up my phone and called the local news channels, one by one. Interviews lined up the following day.

Two days later, a mysterious car appeared behind mine, but my heart held no fear. No one's life would change if I died. Same time as I rounded a turn, his text flashed across my phone: *Be careful.* Deleted.

It was nearly the end of the year. Every day, I'd woken from Heather's nightmares. While running the events on our calendars, be it charity, volunteering, fundraisers, or blogging about women's concerns, we made a pact to travel in clusters. Heather was the evidence of our enemy's power. We possessed no disillusions.

Had it not been for my newfound mission, mourning Heather would have been unbearable.

So today too, Dina, I, and two more Lion-Hearted sisters huddled on the couch with our laptops, our words our weapons.

The bell rang. A simple phenomenon, now alarming for us.

Dina rushed to the door and peered through the peephole before parting. "It's the police," she whispered.

The bell rang again, and I jumped in my seat before marching to the door.

Dina blocked it and shook her head. Her face reddened, and her lips quivered.

I gently pushed her aside and flung open the door.

Outside, Sergeant Lewis, the one who had helped when Heather had disappeared, waited with another cop.

"Let me guess, officers, you have search warrants."

"No, Ms. Everly. We are only here to chat."

At first, I hesitated, pretending I had a choice, but I didn't. The people Heather had hated entered her shrine.

Moments later, we sat across the coffee table from one another, and Dina offered them water.

They declined.

"Ms. Everly, this is Mr. Watney. He is an intern, a new cop. You'll benefit from protection."

I glanced at Dina and back at him. "Excuse me?"

"I have lived my life in regret ever since Heather's body washed ashore. Her uncle—"

"I don't want to talk about him. Why do you think we need protection?"

The intern shifted in his seat. "We don't believe Heather was capable of suicide. The woman was too full of life."

A fat tear fell down my face, and my hands trembled in my lap.

Dina held my shoulder, standing beside me.

Sergeant Lewis clasped his hands. "The ring has to be powerful to bring down Heather. What I don't understand is why they'd want to hurt her. A motive is missing."

I stared at the drawer containing Heather's evidence, digging my nails into my palms. "How can we prove they murdered her? Would a motive help?" My eyelids fluttered.

"Yes, a motive will help. We are also awaiting more autopsy results."

He leaned back, glancing at the intern. "Also, I'm following your interviews. Did you know that Sue Miller is in town and working with the ring?" He shook his head. "I want to correct my wrong, Ms. Everly. Heather would have wanted that. Mr. Watney can be your bodyguard in case the ring comes after you."

A few stutters later, I shook my head. "I'm moved, Sergeant. But I can do this on my own with my sisters' help. You are welcome to check on us or provide us with a number should we need you."

He handed me his business card. "Okay, here's my cell number."

I nodded.

"The sex ring has shredded our department and our town. This stain has tainted all cops' reputations, even the good ones."

He cleared his throat as the intern tightened his lips. "I have a few more questions. Do you mind if I ask them?"

I glanced at Dina and the girls, who had receded to the dining table allowing me to have this conversation. "Sure. Go ahead."

"This is regarding your blog titled 'The Ring of the Dead.' " He pulled out a pen and a piece of paper from his back pocket and narrowed his eyes.

"Go on."

"Are you referring to any specific person running the ring who has feigned a death? Because if that is the case, a simple DNA test will expose it, one I have full authority to run. That would be the end of the ring."

My hands shook. I saw the sandcastles Desiree and I used to build on the lake when she lived with the Everlys in the summer of 1985. The bubblegum cotton candy and the popcorn-flavored ice cream we ate at Lincoln Park filled my palate.

She was the childhood friend I hungered for, one whose death I'd mourned.

How could I just give her away?

"Ms. Everly?" He leaned forward and placed a hand on my shoulder.

And then I saw Heather place a lily behind her left ear with a twinkle in her eyes. "Soon, it'll be the right ear," she'd said.

I hung my head. "Desiree Darlington is now known as Dimples."

"Thank you, Ms. Everly."

CHAPTER 17 – THE KING'S SOUL

"You can't murder a legend."
Mars D. Gill

Jason Barnes and Isabella

His Apartment, Kapaa, HI
Present Day

SHATTERING GLASS rang out from the kitchen. Jason dropped his book and sprang to his feet, dashing to the next room, where Isabella swept up broken shards into a dustpan.

"What happened?"

"I dropped my cup. It's okay though." In her bathrobe, Isabella's hands trembled through the maneuver. "I'm sorry."

Jason filled a new cup of water as she finished cleaning. Strutting to the living room, he handed it to her.

"Thank you." She chose a seat across from him while he retrieved his book from the floor.

She sipped her water like a hot beverage. "I've decided."

"About?"

"Us." She set her cup down.

"Sorry?" He dog-eared a corner of the page and shut the book, holding it close to his chest.

She leaned in and brought her hands together. "I've been thinking, Jason. A lot. I've lain awake in my bed, sat staring at the ocean, just thinking. I've even written it down in my notebook."

"Okay. What is it?" A faint smiled crossed his lips.

"We need to get back together."

His smile faded, and his pitch rose. "Isa—"

She raised her hands. "Jason, let me finish. I don't care you had an affair, and I can tell that you love her. For reasons beyond me but you do. Our boys are hurting, while watching us break apart. Shuffling between Chicago and Hawaii, a good ten hours apart, is far from a normal childhood."

He clenched his teeth. "Isabella, you lied to the police and put me behind bars, and you called Purple Ink, costing me my life's investment, my company—"

"And yet you sit across from me, taking care of me." She tilted her head. "If this isn't love, what is?"

Jason's mouth opened and closed twice, but he could only manage a shake of his head.

"Look, I made a mistake. Losing you messed with my head, and we're helping no one with our fight. Andrew's grades have fallen. Jared's developed a stutter, and Josh's waking every night with terrors—my mom just told me all this."

Her eyes welled up. "They're innocent victims of our failure. I can look past your affair with Anna and only hope that you, too, can get over our court battles and call it even. We can build our lives and our home again and not let our vows be just words." She clasped her hands. "Please, Jason. I'll do anything you ask of me—anything. I can confess to lying to the police."

He slouched in his chair, his book hanging limply from his hands.

"A reason to be unlike your father is no reason at all. You aren't like him. When you left, you remained in touch. Heck, you slammed court cases to fight for the boys. What's wrong with our devotion to our boys being the bond that keeps us together?"

"Nothing," he whispered.

Isabella's eyes sparkled, her body springing forward.

"Except one thing." Jason stared at his book.

"What?" Isabella's shoulders slouched.

"You lied to a dangerous extent, Isabella, and I can't respect that." His face broke into tiny shivers. "You tried to extort money from me when you knew I wouldn't let finances be a problem for you or the boys. You put me in jail for God's sake!"

Still pleading with him, she swayed. "I'm begging for your forgiveness."

Jason shook his head and shuddered, remembering the police escorting him. He set his book on the table and whispered, "And I love Anna."

The color on her face paled as she cleared her throat. "Nothing we can't overcome if we put our heart and soul to it."

"I want to be happy again." His eyes shimmered.

"I'll make you happy, baby."

"You said those words when we married."

"Circumstances of our marriage were such, Jason. Now we have three little hearts to protect. Moving the kids halfway around the world, away from their mother, grandparents, aunts, and uncles is an unfair deal."

Jason opened his mouth, but Isabella brought her chair in front of him, dropped to her knees, and tugged on his hands. "I don't want to hear a yes or a no from you—just think about it. All our lives depend on this, and if I can excuse what I found to be unjustifiable once, maybe you can forgive me too."

Jason's chest heaved. How could they ever bring each other happiness now after years of struggles? Anna, on the other hand, brought him joy just by being present. She enraptured him in her tenacity to fight and take chances, her life anything but ordinary.

Isabella rose, placed her hand on his shoulder, then paraded to the bedroom as Jason hung his head.

He counted to stabilize his heartbeat. On ten, he rose, slid his feet into his sneakers, and blasted out of the house.

Outside, though it was sunny, rain pelted his back. The cool wetness calmed his body through the jog as images flashed in front of his eyes: Isabella wiping tears, holding the subpoenas for their kids. "I know she's left you—we can settle now," she had said. Jason increased his pace. So what if he slipped on the wet trail and headed straight for the ocean below? His muscles crunched as he grimaced, halted, and grabbed his knees, huffing.

To his right, he recognized the shed where he, as Adam, and Anna had spent several moments talking together. He lumbered to its benches, sat, and pulled his phone out of his pocket. Anna had returned none of his messages. Running his tongue over his lips and fighting the urge to flee to her, he fixed his hair. How he missed her perfume, her smile, and her soft skin. With trembling fingers, he browsed the local news app. He gasped and rose alarmed at the headline: Desiree, better known as Dimples, subpoenaed.

A tap on his back made him shudder and jerk around. Behind him stood Sue, her mouth agape.

Anger rose inside his throat as he glared at her, who had forged a friendship with Isabella, brutally attacked Anna, and now had the gall to look him in his eyes. He scowled and passed around her as though she was nobody. While he climbed the hill, Sue followed him.

At the top, she grasped his shoulder. "How's Anna?"

He spun on the spot, gritted his teeth, and punched her face. "Stay away from Anna!"

She fell on the ground.

The rain had ceased, and he dashed toward the villa, his throat collapsing.

What if Anna was right that Isabella and Sue's coming to Kauai together wasn't a coincidence? Shoot!

At the villa, he bounced from foot to foot each second, waiting for someone to answer the door.

When Anna flung it open, instantly he reached for her face, but she extended her hand out for a handshake. Suppressing a smile and licking his lips, he shook her hand, itching to kiss her.

He didn't release her hand and fought her pull. "I'm sorry. You have every right to be angry at me."

"I'm not angry." She smiled an artificial slit in her lips, making her more tempting.

"No?" He raised his brow. "I've missed you like crazy."

"Sure, you have." She pulled her hand away as Jason felt lost without her touch.

"You are angry."

"No, I'm not."

He raised his hand. "We can do this all day. I'm trying tirelessly to manage Isabella. It hasn't been easy."

Anna bit her lip and stared at her feet.

"She's kept me occupied, but I've been following your activity. I'm so proud of you."

"Jason, go back to your wife, okay? You left."

He swallowed hard, his Adam's apple bobbing as he approached her.

She nodded and slammed the door shut in his face. And he stared at the shadow of her feet beneath it, having lost all his bearings, his core pulled out of him. His hand rose and touched the cold door, caressing it as if it were her, his hand the only sane part of his body.

He sighed, knowing what he had to do and worrying about Isabella's wrath or health wasn't it. He couldn't afford to lose Anna again. He turned around and dashed to his home, fists pumping.

When he barged inside, candles shimmered on the dining table. Isabella emerged with a steaming bowl of pasta. "You're back!"

"Yes, what's all this?" He wiped a streak of sweat off his forehead.

"The boys arrive tomorrow." She placed the bowl on the laid-out table, holding copious amounts of food. "Let's make the most of our last night alone."

"You didn't have to go through the trouble."

"Trouble, shmuble. Come on, let's sit and eat. Food's hot."

Jason took the corner seat across from her. Oh, why was she in her favorite bottle-green dress, the one she reserved for most precious occasions. His shoulders drooped. He scanned the table. Spaghetti with meatballs, salad with herb chicken. "Wow!"

Dig in," she ordered sweetly. "And save room for cheesecake afterward."

The silence was deafening. Had he led her astray? He spoke cautiously. "I visited Anna."

"I know."

"What? How?"

"I saw you while jogging on the bike trail." She tipped salad onto her plate. "I'm sure you worry about her."

Jason put his fork down, his dimpled signature smirk plastered on his face. "You saw me? Or you have sources?"

Isabella chuckled.

"Does it not bother you I went to see her?"

"No. You're helping me get over Henry, and I'll help you too."

Where was Isabella's self-respect? "What if I don't want to get over her?" His breaths became heavy. "We separated in mind, spirit, and body over a year ago and overcame the agony and pain surrounding it all. I can't allow that to repeat—you know, on-again, off-again."

She gulped her food. "That wouldn't be good, but did you think about what I said?"

"The arrangement?"

Isabella cleared her throat and wiped her lips with her napkin, hiding a trembling smile. "Love will come after."

"If it didn't come in thirteen years, why would it now?"

Their silence hurt at places too deep in the heart, but no more words existed between them. Jason stared at his plate full of food and whispered, "Do you mind if I leave this unfinished?"

"Why would a plate bother me when it's our lives you are leaving unfinished?"

He rose, marched to his bedroom, and started to pack.

Through the opening in the door, Isabella played with her food before picking up her phone.

He stopped folding his clothes.

"You are good to go" she said into the receiver.

He dropped his shirt. Who had she just called? Did she continue to conjure against the woman he loved?

Life without Jason

Hawaii
Present Day

MY LIFE CONDENSED into a capsule of fog. Concentrating was tough. The trapped bird called my soul had stopped struggling to break free. Loveless, I'd resigned. Jason had assumed the role of a well-wisher when I hungered him to be the hero of my broken life. So, everywhere I traveled, I wasn't supposed to be. Orphaned by Heather's death, I longed for her hearty laugh that vibrated the floor. And her complaints. I would pay to hear one. Shrouded by thoughts, I visited places. Today, I shopped for a fundraiser.

Only the voice of the cashier alerted me of my whereabouts.

"That'll be one hundred and nineteen dollars and twenty-two cents," the checkout lady said.

I handed her the cash while noticing her protruding belly. "How far along?"

"Any day now. It's my third. Do you have any kids?"

I did . . . My eyelids dropped. "No."

I toddled outside with my bags, where sun's brisk rays assaulted my eyes while I loaded my car's trunk. My phone rang for the sixth time with an unknown number. I dismissed it and hopped into the car.

Pulling out of the parking lot, I contemplated going to the villa full of people. The women Heather had helped showed up constantly to volunteer. Babies were being born, a lady with a child now lived with us, and someone always occupied our couch. People sympathized with Heather's last cause and were angry at what the "secret" sex ring had done to the moral tenet of their community.

I sighed. A strange heaviness stung me, the same I had lugged around at the East Coast Writers Conference or while writing the letters to Jason.

It hurt so bad my heart grew numb. I swerved away from the villa, wondering about the purpose of it all.

Heather's voice reverberated in my soul. "That cross section is cursed by the spirit of King Kaumualii. Bad things happen there all the time, and we must lift the curse."

I zipped along the curvaceous mountain, and a memory emerged: the wild wind lifting my hair, my red lips slipping into a smile, a happy song erupting in my head, and the rental bicycle clicking into a rhythmic beat.

I veered off to a side alley, and the tires screeched. I knew where I had to go.

Sue Miller

Antique Shop, Kapaa, HI
Present Day

SUE'S HEART HAD SHRUNK, her life capsized as she placed a china doll on the top shelf. Boring as an adverb-littered manuscript, she too hung onto meaning with poor props like Desiree. Perched atop a ladder, her gaze fell on Anna marching toward her. Her heart missed a beat, and her hands trembled as she descended the rungs.

Anna halted and clutched her chest as Sue scurried to her.

Her color pale, Anna jabbed her finger at Sue. "The letters lay inside my floral bag around my neck, and when I'd turned, I'd seen something or someone familiar, and then, I hit a boulder."

Sue glanced around. "Okaaay. But why are you here now?"

"To buy antiques, of course." Anna squinted.

Sue grabbed her hand, then yanked her into a side hallway, and out the back door.

Anna allowed her.

"I saw you right before I fell."

"What?"

"October 2, 2013." Anna tapped on Sue's shoulder with her index finger.

"You did see me but after you fell."

"What?" Anna pulled on her hair.

Sue put her hands forward. "Listen, we can't afford to be seen together."

To Sue's surprise, Anna's frown ceased, her eyes filled up, and her hands dropped low to each side. "Sue, what do you have against me?" Her voice cracked.

Sue bit her bottom lip and glanced around again, her eyes fluttering.

"How could I ever have anything against you? If your memory had returned, you would know I have foolishly loved you." She wiped a tear. "Now Olivia has left me too . . ."

"Why are you here with Desiree?" Anna folded her arms.

A smile flashed past her lips, and Sue adjusted the frame on her glasses and whispered, "I'm your guardian angel."

"What?"

She led Anna further away from the shop to another door. "You saw Desiree before your accident. She was supposed to be dead, and you must've been in shock."

"Or you could be lying."

Sue pinched her ears. "It's my best guess, I swear. I found you on the ground after a car sped past. Desiree sat inside with a man. I—"

A commotion erupted in the shop. "Where's Sue?" Mrs. Parker's voice shouted.

"Oh, snap!" Sue opened the back door and pulled Anna into a dingy storeroom, basking in red light. Piles of paperwork littered the desk. Hastily, she bolted it. "The day Heather left you—"

"Left?"

"Yes, listen, I don't have time. Desiree and I visited Heather that day."

Sue had cringed as Heather had grabbed her by the collars at the villa's entrance with Desiree behind her.

"You hurt my daughter!" she had yelled.

Desiree broke Heather away. "Listen, Ms. Hiwalani, we didn't come here to fight. Please let's talk inside. It's business."

"I recognize you from somewhere?" Heather narrowed her eyes.

Sue jolted. "L-let's get to the point. Where's Anna?"

"Who are you?" Heather opened the door.

"Yes, I'm Dimples. I hear you run a safe house for women."

"I do. Do you need help, dear?" Heather rested her hand on Desiree as Sue had squirmed.

Desiree laughed, entering the villa through the open door. "No but thank you for asking. What services do you provide?"

Sue followed, trembling and shutting the door behind them.

As Desiree sat, Heather took a seat across from her. "I help women find employment and stand on their two feet. When they need protection from life's cruelties like domestic abuse, etc., I protect them."

Sue grabbed the backside of Desiree's chair, standing behind her.

Desiree crossed her legs. "Right. I do the same thing."

"Pardon me?"

"Just like you, I help women find lucrative professions, get independent, and lead healthy lifestyles." She pointed at Sue.

"Do you?" Heather raised her brow.

"Yes. Would you like to work for me?"

Heather's big frame shook under an involuntary chuckle. "In what capacity?"

"If your girls are looking for employment and get independent, send them my way." She handed Heather her card.

"Heavenly Escapes, behind the novel antique shop in Kapaa." She reared her head above the card. "What kind of jobs do you offer?"

"All levels, from management to admins, waitresses, entertainers—"

"Entertainers?"

Sue crossed her arms.

"What kind of entertainers? Do they perform for a circus or what?"

"Life is a circus, Ms. Hiwalani. We sell everything from songs to alternate realities."

"Alternate realities? Who do you entertain?" She furrowed her brow.

"Primarily men."

"Oh." Heather crossed her arms.

"Oh? Is there a problem?"

"No." She turned to Sue. "Is that what you do there, Sue?"

"No. I take care of the shop." Sue's lips trembled as she stared at her feet.

"Ms. Hiwalani, is there a problem?" Desiree rose.

"No, you came to the right place because I can bring you a lot of business." She nodded. "Very smart."

"Wonderful! Let's fill out the paperwork—non-disclosure forms, etc., shall we?"

"Now?" Heather scratched her forehead.

Desiree cocked at Heather with a smirk. "Are you having second thoughts, Ms. Hiwalani?"

"No, not at all. Where are we going?"

"To heaven."

I slumped in a chair, holding my mouth. "Why did you take her to Heather?"

Sue rolled her eyes. "I had to win her trust so I could unite you two—"

"You two?"

"You and Desiree. You came to Hawaii searching for her. I wanted to help. How could I predict Heather would move in with us? Y—" Steady footfalls from outside the door halted Sue's words. "You must leave," she whispered, shaking her head and clutching her throat.

"Not until you tell me what happened to Heather." I leaned forward. "Sue?"

She held her head and paced. "I thought she would sign the paperwork and leave. The next day I walked in on her in this very room." She pointed to the desk. "She stood right there behind that table, and three policemen were trembling where we are."

"What?" I rose.

Steadying herself, grabbing onto the desk, she whispered hoarsely, "She was on a revenge mission, taking on a bigger role with Desiree. They provide lodging here like Heather's safe house, except it's not safe." Sue squeezed my hands, her eyes unblinking. "They hurt her, and with your public interviews, they'll do to you what they did to Heather. It's a filthy business, but don't worry. I support your mission to end this ring. Carry on, and I'll fight here from the inside."

My eyes welled up, blurring Sue's frame. "Why? What's in it for you?"

She chuckled sadly. "An old habit, Anna, of looking after you." She released my hands. "Don't worry about me."

"I'm sorry." I took her in a big hug, and her body trembled. "You are a good person, Sue and so easily misunderstood. I thought you had contrived with Isabella."

She pulled away, wiping a tear. "I did, I did but not to harm you. I have always intended to protect you." Without looking into my eyes, she opened the door and disappeared into the hallway leading to the shop.

I lingered a moment before leaving.

I now knew how to lift the King's soul and break his curse. Meeting with Sue freed a load off me, burst her dark cloud that had swirled over my head. I stayed away from the ring, only using my blogs as vessels carrying the truths Heather had wanted to share. I remained in touch with Sergeant Lewis. Rumors started swirling, and debates took place on local news.

Then came the morning when the DNA matched, and the police arrested Desiree and Mrs. Parker. With the ring shut down, I felt Heather's spirit lift in peace.

Desiree was right: Everything came with a price. To bring Heather justice, I had paid the ultimate cost of giving up my childhood friend. She had left me for dead on the mountainside. Had it not been for Sue, I wouldn't be alive.

Right after the news of the ring, I called Sue to accompany me to Kōke'e, the place where it all began.

The Peace Offering

Kōke‘e Mountains, Kauai, Hawaii
December 2014

THE KEHAU WINDS whistled and howled. Everything glistened in a wet glaze of rain, and rainbows painted the sky. One moment, the clouds rumbled and poured; in another moment, the sun sparkled across drenched roads. Sue parked along the road illegally. Our business was as quick as my accident. The gusts of wind tousled our hair and thrashed our clothes.

She marched past the boulder along the side of the cliff with a stick and drew a circle on the mud. "This is where I found you."

I entered it. Sue opened a bag and pulled out an assortment of old items.

First came my jacket soiled with jelly from the conference, the one Sue had retrieved. Next, she drew out a bottle-green dress.

"What's this?"

"It's Isabella's—her truce. Did you bring the letters?"

"No," I whispered and stared at my feet. I didn't have the heart to burn the letters. Once written, words forever left our ownership and belonged to someone else.

"Okay, whatever." She shook her head, " *'A'ohe—*"

"In English, please."

"No cliff is too tall to be climbed."

She recited more local verses, and I fought the slashing winds to stay inside the circle.

We sought permission to live as though we'd never hurt each other, but a deeper meaning endured within this ritual: what beat in our hearts but departed our lives. Heather's spirit.

When Sue finished, I pulled out a lighter from my purse, flicked it on, and threw it on the pile. The wind fought the extinguishing flames. Five attempts later, a fireball shot up, and I gasped.

"Quick, get out!" shouted Sue.

I stared at the green dress blackened into cinders, my eyes moistening into an ocean.

"Get out!" She shrieked as the flames heated my cheeks.

I ducked and strode out of the circle. Outside, Sue and I held hands tightly, wiping our tears until only ash hovered over the mountain and inside our nostrils.

Moments later, Sue dropped me off at the summit. That was the last time I saw her.

At the summit, I passed a rooster in the parking lot while music blazed out of a standing car. Tourists clung to Kōke'e as bees darted from flower to flower.

When I reached the end of the mountain, the wetness from the surrounding clouds tickled my cheeks. How did the sunlight paint the ocean blue when clouds could touch my face? The air cooled my ash-smeared throat. I breathed in and out. A gentle compression on my shoulder brought the knowledge of his presence. As I'd burned my superstitions, Jason had hiked those same trails. We faced the ocean without uttering a word. The chatter of tourists didn't reach my ears, only the whistling Kehau winds and the rustling of his shirt.

His hand brushed mine before he grabbed it tightly. At the place where it all began, we held hands, only letting the silence speak. So what if more challenges awaited us? So what if his complicated life wouldn't untangle just because I'd reached the summit of mine? We had endured a lifetime of trials.

We strolled to the parking lot where Jason slid into the passenger seat of the car he'd driven, Heather's car.

I'd worry about the upcoming challenges later. This present day was mine. I was free, and my curses had lifted. I'd embodied the core spirit of Hiwalani Keahi—leaving the summit with him. Just how I had meandered down the mountain with hands outstretched, humming a carefree tune, today, too, I sat next to him in the car, my heart fluttering like a butterfly. We uttered no words, just carried two happy hearts. For all the people we had lost in the last year, nothing could erase what we had gained.

The road slipped beneath us as the ocean shimmered, and our car became a dot down in the valley. And that was all we were: a dot in the grand scheme of things.

NOT THE END

ACKNOWLEDGEMENT

I drew my strength from the following hearts. Thank you to:

My *husband*, my *children*, and my *parents* for grounding me and being there for me.

The person who has read all my books, including this one, when my work was objectionably crude: *Rosamin Bhanpuri*.

Jasmine Dhaliwal, my best friend, for being my soul whisperer, nourishing me with a constant dose of encouragement, and proofreading this book.

Debbie Leonard Klein and *Helene Mell Dunn* for critiquing this book twice.

Glenda Thompson for beta reading and giving honest feedback.

Rachelle M. N. Shaw for line and copy editing. What sets her apart is her humble delivery of feedback, her honest desire to help fellow authors, and her keen eye for catching writing mistakes.

Pam Humphrey, fellow author, for guiding me every step of the way.

Hitpreet Raheja for guiding me in building my writers platform.

Gratitude is the memory of the heart
~ Jean Baptiste Massieu

About the Author

MARS D. GILL is the author of her debut novel *Letters from the Queen*. Her upcoming work features a Women's Fiction debut named Land of Dreams which centers on a young, Punjabi American girl, Siana Singh. Her father had lovingly termed America as the Land of Dreams until one day he is shot dead in a random crime. Now Siana must discover the meaning behind those words by pursuing his unrealized dreams. But can she when she is unable to forgive the killer? This follows an unnamed novel that transports love from interior streets of New Delhi and the US to the outer space. Stay tuned for her future releases by signing up for her newsletters at: **www.bookofdreams.us** or her author page in Facebook – Book of Dreams – Mars D. Gill Books.

She is also open to select readings and lectures. To inquire about a possible appearance, please contact her at bookofdreams.us@gmail.com.

www.ingramcontent.com/pod-product-compliance
Lightning Source LLC
Chambersburg PA
CBHW021135110726
47900CB00002B/368